High-speed rescue

Racing alongside, Alec saw Billy's saddle suddenly slip from beneath him! Now Gunfire was in full racing stride and Billy was half off, his feet tangled in the loose stirrup irons.

Alec pulled the Black over to the free-running gelding and grabbed Billy's shoulders, holding him until the jockey righted himself. Even then he couldn't take away his support, for the saddle had slipped underneath Gunfire and the stirrups were dangling dangerously close to his legs. If they tripped him, he'd go down, and Billy's only chance of escape would be to hang on to Alec—if the Black didn't go down too.

The Black Stallion Series
by Walter Farley

The Black Stallion
The Black Stallion Returns
Son of the Black Stallion
The Island Stallion
The Black Stallion and Satan
The Black Stallion's Blood Bay Colt
The Island Stallion's Fury
The Black Stallion's Filly
The Black Stallion Revolts
The Black Stallion's Sulky Colt
The Island Stallion Races
The Black Stallion's Courage
The Black Stallion Mystery
The Horse-Tamer
The Black Stallion and Flame
Man o' War
The Black Stallion Challenged!
The Black Stallion's Ghost
The Black Stallion and the Girl
The Black Stallion Legend
The Young Black Stallion (with Steven Farley)

The Black Stallion's Courage

WALTER FARLEY

Bullseye Books • Alfred A. Knopf • New York

For Timothy

Contents

Old Mare, Young Man

1

Alec Ramsay opened his eyes and stared into the darkness of his bedroom. He could not sleep. The darkness was familiar enough, but not the complete silence that lay over everything.

Long moments passed and he could *hear* the stillness. It was more than the hush, the quiet of late night. It was more than the complete absence of sound. It was a vibrant, living silence and he listened to it as one would to the soft rustle of leaves in the stir of air. He listened to it while his eyes opened again, searching the darkness—for *what?*

Suddenly he swung out of bed and went to the open east window. If he couldn't sleep, the thing to do was to get up and find out what was the matter. He put his head out the window, listening to the stillness. If he wasn't mistaken, it meant trouble. Something was going to break fast. It was the quiet before the storm, the quiet that preceded an onslaught of terrible force. Where would it come from? What would it be?

Just beyond the stallion barn were the separate paddocks and in one he saw Napoleon's white, ghostlike figure. The old gelding was standing still, probably asleep. Somewhere in the adjacent paddock was the Black.

The boy's keen eyes searched the darkness for some sign of movement. Finally they found the tall stallion, his head up and the pricked ears showing clearly against the backdrop of stars. The Black did not move. The night remained still, too still.

Alec's gaze swept across the fields to where the mares and suckling foals were grazing. He made out their dark movements but heard nothing except the silence, so heavy with its dreadful portent. If the danger was not to come from the Black would the mares be the ones to set it off?

Turning from the window, Alec went to the closet and pulled on a pair of coveralls over his pajamas. The only thing to do was to go out and look things over. Some of the new broodmares didn't get along very well together. Also, old Miz Liz was due to foal sometime soon and it just might be tonight. She'd bear watching. If Snappy, the foaling man, was on the job, Alec wouldn't have to worry about her.

Softly Alec tiptoed to the door, carrying his boots so as not to wake up his parents. Then he remembered that he would need his house key to get back in, and retraced his steps to the closet. The key should be in his brown suit. The last time he'd used it was two weeks ago when he'd seen Henry off on the train for Pimlico racetrack. He missed having his old partner and trainer around the farm.

He found the key and something else which he had completely forgotten about—a registered letter that he'd picked up at the local post office after leaving Henry. Concerned and angered at his forgetfulness, he went to a small desk and switched on the lamp. The letter was from the insurance company. Opening it he found that as of three days ago, when final payment on the fire insurance policy had been due, all the barns and other buildings of Hopeful Farm were unprotected in case of loss or damage! Furious with himself, Alec shoved the letter into his pocket. It was inexcusable that he should have forgotten to give the premium notice to his father, allowing the policy to lapse.

He left his bedroom and went quietly down the hall, stopping only at his father's business office. There he left the letter on the big desk, knowing that he'd have a lot of explaining to do later in the morning.

Outside the house he waited a moment until his eyes became accustomed to the darkness. Again he heard the stillness and felt its warning. This was very real. This was not his imagination playing tricks with him.

Having the lapsed insurance policy heavy on his mind, he thought back to the warning he had given Snappy about smoking in the broodmare barn. Twice during the past week he'd had to speak sharply to the foaling man about it. More apprehensive than ever, Alec now started running down the road while behind him the Black snorted, breaking the deathly quiet of the night.

Going into the dimly lit broodmare barn, Alec breathed deeply the odors he loved—the hay, ammonia and feed. He smelled no tobacco smoke. He walked down the long corridor of empty box stalls, going toward the far end of the barn where he'd find Miz Liz all by herself in the biggest stall of all awaiting the birth of her colt or filly. It wouldn't be to-night, Alec decided, or Snappy would have had the place more brightly lit.

At the large foaling stall, Alec peeked over the half-door. Miz Liz stood beneath a very small overhead bulb, looking fat and tired, with her head drooped.

"Hello, old mare," Alec said softly, going into the stall. There was only a slight twitching of Miz Liz's long ears to disclose she'd heard him.

Alec squinted, deepening the white creases in skin as tanned as old saddle leather, while he examined the mare. He looked at her longer than was necessary, remembering Henry's description of her going to the post as a three-year-old, all sleek and shiny and fired up, so long ago. Running his hand over the mare's sagging back, Alec left the stall.

Now he thought he knew the ominous portent of the night's stillness. Miz Liz was going to foal very soon and that spelled trouble. Where was Snappy?

Alec opened the door of the small room beside the foaling stall. There were a chair and a cot, both empty. The foaling equipment was set out with the oxygen tank ready for use if necessary. It was Snappy's job to be here *now,* watching Miz Liz. It could happen any moment.

Leaving the room, Alec stood in the corridor. Suddenly he heard the faint sound of music. He looked up at the ceiling, certain that Snappy was in Henry's vacant apartment, where he had no right to be at any time, much less tonight. With a bound Alec climbed the stairs, taking two at a jump. Reaching the apartment door, he flung it open without knocking and there was Snappy sitting in Henry's big living-room chair, his feet on the center table and a pipe in his mouth. Mixed with the pleasant aroma of burning tobacco was the hickory-wood smell of smoked bacon frying on the kitchen stove!

Startled by the opening of the door, Snappy looked up and then quickly removed his long legs from the table.

Alec said, "You're sure making yourself at home while Henry's away."

The man mumbled something beneath his breath and then said, "I figured he wouldn't mind."

"You know he minds. It's his home and he likes to keep it private, the same as you would. He's told you that before."

The man banged his pipe bowl against a white saucer, knocking out the top ashes; then he relit the tobacco.

Alec went on. "Just as we've warned you before about smoking in the barn."

"This is Henry's apartment," the man said curtly, "not the barn."

"It's the same thing, and Henry doesn't smoke."

"You're not tellin' me nothin'. He's too old to have any bad habits. He ain't worth much any more, Henry ain't. Anybody can see that."

For several minutes Alec didn't answer. Knowing he'd gone too far, Snappy shifted uneasily in the chair. "I won't burn your farm down," he said. "You don't have to worry none. Just go back to sleep and forget you found me here. I'll take care of my end, all right."

Alec saw the grin on the man's thick lips but he ignored it just as he did Snappy's outspoken arrogance. Good foaling men were hard to find and Snappy was one of the best. Hopeful Farm needed such a man.

"I want you downstairs," Alec said finally, holding his temper. "Miz Liz is going to foal."

"Not right this minute she ain't. Too much rushin' and

hurryin' only causes those old mares trouble. Let her be."
The big man smiled, reassured of his position. "Besides, I
got this pipeful to finish."

Alec broke out all over in clammy perspiration and his
hands trembled. "With some mares you can wait," he said,
"but not with her. You should know better than I that it's
too dangerous."

"If you're worried, go take care of her yourself," the man
answered. "I don't need this job. I got people wantin' me
back home, lots of people. Plenty of mares in Kentucky but
not many foaling men like me."

"Only because your father was the greatest of all teachers,"
Alec said, unable to control himself any longer. "Everybody
knows that. But I don't think you ever listened to him,
Snappy. If you had you wouldn't be sitting here smoking a
pipe when Miz Liz is about to foal! So you're not good
enough for our farm any longer. You're fired, Snappy. Now
get out of here and stay out!" He reached for the man's arm.

Snappy rose and towered above Alec, the pipe smoke curl-
ing about his surprised but scornful eyes. Then his big hands
tore Alec's fingers away from his arm and he gave the boy a
hard push.

Although Alec braced himself for the backward fall, his
head hit the floor with terrific impact. And although he did
not lose consciousness he was barely aware of Snappy's leaving the apartment.

Alec lay on the floor a short while, waiting for his head to
clear. Then, suddenly, he heard a loud snort from below. He
struggled to his feet and opened the apartment door, shouting down the stairwell to Miz Liz that she was not alone
with her foal! He knew the foal had come, that he had only a
few seconds more to reach the stall in time to prevent what

he dreaded. Miz Liz always got to her feet soon after foaling. It wouldn't be any different this time. That's why Snappy should have been there, waiting.

Running down the stairs, Alec made straight for the end of the corridor, where he flipped on the bright overhead light. The foaling stall came to life with festive brilliance. In the center Miz Liz was climbing to her feet, while beside her deep in the straw lay her newly born colt.

Alec did not stay quietly outside the stall to watch mother and son become acquainted in those wondrous first moments together as he did with other mares. Instead he flung open the door and shouted! Miz Liz moved toward her colt, not to lick his coat dry *but to kill him*!

Alec reached out and slapped her hindquarters hard, throwing her off balance and distracting her attention. Startled, she hesitated before the sight of his raised hand and the sound of his urgent commands.

The mare's eyes were wild, matching the viciousness shown by her flattened ears. Yet she fell back a step, giving Alec a chance to gather the wet colt in his arms. She came for them when the boy moved toward the door, her head outstretched and teeth bared.

Alec swung the colt away from her and felt the searing pinch of her teeth as she turned upon him in all her fury and frustration. But she had not taken hold and he jumped through the open door, slamming it behind him.

Gently he placed the newly born foal on the floor, while the stall became suddenly quiet. Left alone, Miz Liz would cause no trouble. For a moment Alec looked at her as she stood so wearily beneath the bright light, her wet coat matted with straw and manure. She showed no further interest in him or her colt, not even when the boy spoke to her.

"Old mare, why do you make these moments, which should be the best of all, so terrible? I'm not going to let you kill him as you did another of your sons. Nor will you kill me as you did old Charley Grimm. I'm not afraid of you, old mare, just very sad for you."

He turned to the sprawled bundle on the floor, all legs and head and eyes. A fine colt. Not black like his famous sire but chestnut with a blaze, the same as Miz Liz. A big-boned colt. Big nostrils, too. Good for scooping in the air on his way down the homestretch when he'd need it most.

Alec's hands were slippery on the wet body. Large eyes, so inquisitive and unafraid, met his own. Finally he rose and went to the adjacent room, noting the equipment he'd need later on. Taking a soft, clean cloth he went back to the colt and began wiping him dry.

"Not the same as your mother's tongue," he said, "but it'll do for the time being."

For many minutes he watched the colt's attempts to un-limber the long forelegs that would not do what he asked of them. It wouldn't take long before this fellow would be the master of his gangling body.

"I hate to tell you this," Alec said, picking up the colt once more, "but you don't have a very smart mother. At first she doesn't know you and won't have you. In fact, she'd like to do away with you. But after a while, not so very long from now, she'll come over to us very slowly and we won't have to run away. She'll put her old head down and sniff, and then she'll start licking you, just as though none of this had happened at all."

He opened the stall door, still talking to the colt. "My job will be done then and she'll be as loving as she is mean now. But as I said she's not very smart at the beginning. We have to keep reminding her that you're hers and there's no getting out of it."

Miz Liz had moved to the corner of her stall. She stood quietly, showing no interest in them, her disheveled head hung low. Alec shifted the heavy, awkward bundle in his arms so he might watch her better. He did not move far from the door while letting the colt support some of his own weight.

"Old mare," he called, "this is your son, and the sooner you get to know him the sooner I can clean you up and get this business over with. But I'll not come a step closer. I know you too well."

Without raising her head, Miz Liz suddenly plunged toward them, her nostrils flared and ears back. Alec pulled the colt outside and slammed the stall door in the mare's face. She made no attempt to reach over it but turned and went back to the corner of her stall again.

Breathing heavily, Alec put down the colt. "Anyway, she's getting to know you," he said. "It shouldn't take too much longer."

Far down the corridor the door banged open and his father's running figure emerged from the darkness. "Dad, what are you doing here?" Alec called.

His father didn't need to answer. He opened the door leading upstairs and smoke billowed into the corridor! Only then did Alec remember with horror that Snappy had been frying bacon on Henry's stove—and that he had forgotten to turn it off!

No longer was the night still. When Alec ran toward the stairs to help his father he heard the crackling of flames beyond the smoke. The onslaught of destruction had come and he had helped to create it.

Fiery Aftermath

2

The smoke rose above the barn . . . softly, moving, waving, drifting. Then with a deafening roar the night was shattered by the raging inferno that had spawned the smoke. Long tongues of flame reached out from second-story windows, greedily grasping and devouring adjacent treetops. Echoing the scream of the fire came the snorts and squeals of pastured horses. From farther away came the wailing siren of the village firehouse, summoning its volunteers.

Inside the barn Alec and his father came down the stairs from the second floor, their figures seeming to float through the dim, murky veil of heat.

"Get the colt, Dad," the boy said. "We've done all we can up there." There was no fright in his voice, only defeat. "I'll take the mare." He picked up an empty feed sack.

Mr. Ramsay nodded but his eyes were glazed and staring as if he didn't understand at all. Yet he went to the colt and picked him up carefully, steadying him on his feet. Then he turned to Alec and the glassiness left his eyes. "You'd better be careful of her, son."

He watched Alec step inside the stall, talking to Miz Liz as if nothing at all were happening upstairs. His voice was so soft that Mr. Ramsay could catch a word only now and then, but by watching the frightened mare he knew she was listening to Alec. He moved along the corridor, the colt heavy in his arms.

Alec snapped the lead shank onto Miz Liz's halter and wrapped the sack about her head so she could not see. "Come," he whispered, starting her toward the door. With the roar above and the heat in her flared nostrils, Miz Liz was no longer vicious, only terribly afraid. Neither he nor the colt had anything to fear from her now, thought Alec. But what a price to pay for their acceptance!

Suddenly the ceiling directly above them exploded and slender bits of flame fell at Alec's feet, igniting the straw. He and the mare leaped as one through the stall door and into the corridor.

Now the very air was alive with tiny particles of heat that stung Alec's face. He pulled down the mare's head, shielding it as best he could with his own body. Only once did he look up, and he saw a raging canopy of fire directly above them. He hurried Miz Liz along the corridor faster, for in her new terror she was inclined to hang back. More and more falling tongues of flame were coming down now and Alec began twisting as he ran in an effort to avoid them. Miz Liz screamed and bolted forward in pain. Fortunately the exit was just ahead and they followed Mr. Ramsay and the colt through it and out into the coolness of the night air.

They stayed at a run until Alec could no longer feel the heat upon his back, and then he slowed Miz Liz. He removed the blindfold and she stood trembling beside him for a few minutes; finally she whinnied. He rubbed her muzzle, knowing that her soft utterance wasn't for him or for joy at the fresh, clean air in her nostrils. No, it was for her son, who had been placed on the grass beside the road and was now the center of her attention.

Mr. Ramsay was looking back at the fire. "Oh, Alec," he said in a forlorn wail.

But Alec did not turn and look back. There was nothing anyone could do. Nobody could save a barn full of hay and straw once it started to go. The small water pump and hose which some of the hired men already had hooked up to the adjacent field pond were of little use. So was the fire engine which he could hear coming down the country road. All the pastured horses were safe, but the barn which he and Henry and his father had had built with such pride would be completely destroyed. He did not want to look upon the horror of its burning. Instead he watched the start of a new life.

There were new trials to be watched, too, for the colt was attempting once again to make his forelegs behave. There, there, he had them in place. Eager and strong in his confidence he pulled up his hind legs until they too were where they should be. Then he stood in all his freshly won glory, his eyes bright and seeking, his sharp-ribbed body teetering on stilted legs.

"He's made it, Dad," Alec said, "all by himself."

There was no comment from Mr. Ramsay.

Miz Liz tugged on the lead shank and Alec let her go to her son, watching as she licked him with all the care and tenderness that he'd been missing. It didn't matter that his red, furry coat was perfectly dry, even singed in spots. No, what was important was the reassurance that she was giving him. At last he knew that he was loved and wanted.

Out of the darkness came the close scream of the fire engine. Alec heard his father say bitterly, "Even when I called them, I knew it was too late."

"They can keep it from spreading," Alec said.

"Nothing to spread to," his father answered. "There's no wind to carry the sparks. The other barns are far enough away."

"I was thinking of the trees," Alec said while he steadied the colt, holding him close to the mare. "You'd better eat," he told the colt. "You've waited a long time."

Only when the colt finally was nursing did Alec turn and look at the fire. His eyes became blurred as he gazed upon the blinding spectacle of white and golden fury. Too late even to save the bordering trees, he saw. But they hadn't lost a single horse—not even Miz Liz's colt.

He heard the Black's blasting, repeated whistles but he did not turn toward the far paddock. His eyes were fastened on the sweeping, golden brightness that reached ever higher into the sky. All they'd lost was a barn—their biggest and best barn, but only a barn. Cost? About one hundred thousand dollars *and uninsured.* A total loss. That was all they'd lost, he concluded grimly.

After a while Ed Henne, the fire chief, stood beside him. "I'm awfully sorry, Alec," he said. "We're hooking up our pump to the pond but we won't save much."

"I know, Ed. Thanks, anyway."

The fire burned brightly until dawn while neighbors came and went, some only to watch the fiery spectacle and others to offer their sympathy as well. During one of those long hours his mother stood beside Alec, sharing his loss. She said, "It could have been so much worse, Alec. What if

Henry had been at home and asleep? Think how horrible that would have been! Remember, too, that you've lost none of your horses and there's the insurance to cover the barn."

He hadn't told his mother how wrong she was. If Henry had been at home there'd have been no fire. And there was no insurance. He hadn't wanted to worry her about the lapsed policy then, with the fire so bright in her face.

The roar of lashing, leaping flames died with the gray light of day. The last of the spectators left and then finally the fire truck. There was nothing more to be seen or done. The barn lay black and gutted with only the two stone end walls standing.

"What are you going to do, Alec?" Mr. Ramsay asked, searching the eyes of his son. They hadn't been a youth's eyes for several years, he realized. Too much had happened to Alec. Too many quick decisions had been made in his young life. Too many fast horses had been ridden.

Turning from the water-sodden debris that was all that was left of their broodmare barn, Alec said, "It's not as if it was winter and we couldn't get along without it for a while. The mares and colts can use the field sheds for shelter. We'll keep Miz Liz and her colt in the yearling barn for a few days and then turn them out with the others."

His father nodded. "We'll have the new barn up long before cold weather sets in."

"We will if I can raise the money to rebuild it," Alec said quietly.

His father turned to him, bewildered. "You don't have to worry about that, Alec," he said. "Our insurance covers the barn for the full amount. It's for a hundred thousand dollars, I think. I'll check the policy right away, and put in our claim for payment."

"There's no insurance, Dad. The policy lapsed three days ago."

"I-it what? . . . You mean? . . . How do you know, Alec?"

"I just put the premium notice on your desk tonight. I've had it for the past two weeks."

"You mean you forgot to give it to me?" Mr. Ramsay asked.

Alec nodded miserably. "I left it in my suit pocket."

Mr. Ramsay turned and looked at the gutted building. Finally he said, "It's as much my fault as yours. I should have made note of the renewal date. No notice from the company should have been necessary."

Alec watched the group of mares and colts grazing near the fence. "How much money do we have left of Black Minx's Kentucky Derby purse?" he asked after a few minutes.

"Enough to get a bulldozer to clear the debris away," Mr. Ramsay answered. "Most of the money went to pay off the contractor for the training track. We're not rich at the present time, Alec."

Alec's eyes were drawn to two colts who rose squealing on their hind legs in rough play. "All our money whinnies," he answered quietly.

"You're not thinking of selling any of them?"

"Not if I can help it."

"We might borrow on them," Mr. Ramsay suggested tentatively.

"I'd rather not do that either. We're enough in debt as it is."

"Then what's the alternative?"

"To race."

"Of course, Black Minx," Mr. Ramsay said quickly and simply. "I should have thought of her immediately. But then you and Henry have told me so little of her chances in the coming Preakness. I suppose what she did in the Kentucky Derby she can do again. Beating all those three-year-old colts, I mean. She ought to win the Preakness and the Belmont without too much trouble."

For the first time that night Alec smiled. "That's the most unhorsemanlike statement I've ever heard."

"I've never claimed to be a horseman but I'd like to know what's wrong with my suggesting that she'll win all three big races?" his father asked.

"Only eight horses since 1875 have done it," Alec explained. "And never a filly."

"Well, fillies weren't supposed to win the Kentucky Derby either," Mr. Ramsay said, *"but she did."*

"I know, but it's going to be different from now on."

"You mean you've lost confidence in her, Alec? After all, you should know her better than anyone else, since you ride her. And you flew down to Pimlico to work her this past week."

"She's got the speed and stamina to do it," Alec said. "But I don't know, it's—"

"I don't see what you're worrying about," his father interrupted. "What you need to do is to join Henry at once and make *sure* Black Minx gets a part of those big purses even if she doesn't win. Meanwhile, I'll start getting bids from building contractors on the new barn. There's no sense moaning over our loss. We'll get busy and make up for it, that's what we'll do."

"I'll have to do more than that," Alec said quietly.

"More? You needn't worry about us here. There's plenty

of help and Miz Liz was the last mare to foal."

"I know," Alec said. "I meant that I have to make doubly sure we come back with enough money for the barn."

His father nodded. "If you feel that way, I don't see how you and Black Minx can miss," he said confidently.

"I think it's going to take more than her to do it," Alec answered. "So the Black's going along with me."

A hush came over the early dawn. Even the mares and foals stopped their grazing and play to watch the boy walk up the road toward the tall black stallion who awaited him.

The Racetrack

3

The following Saturday a widely syndicated sportswriter had an interesting column for his readers. It ran as follows:

SPORTS

By "Count" Cornwell

DEADLY DUO

BALTIMORE, MD., May 22—One of the country's most popular young riders will arrive at old Pimlico racetrack this morning but the folks here won't be paying much attention to him. They'll be too busy looking at his horse.

This statement is based on reports received from the special railroad car which is returning the Black to the races. Everywhere the train has stopped, crowds have gathered to look into the car, their eyes so bug-eyed at sight of the famous stallion that they have completely ignored the boy at his side, Alec Ramsay. No animal has ever enjoyed such a triumphant journey to or from a racetrack. The Black's ride will end this morning on a railroad siding at Pimlico, where he'll get down to work.

There will be fanfare here too, of course, but of a drastically different kind. The eyes of professional horsemen will be scrutinizing the Black, looking for signs of his having filled up in front, as retired stallions usually do, and for heavy quarters that would weight him down—both of which would handicap him in his comeback. They know that the older a horse gets the harder it is to bring him back to winning form, and most of them say they wouldn't want the job *even with the Black*!

But Hopeful Farm's trainer, Henry Dailey, isn't listening to anyone but himself. He's convinced that the Black can be brought back and will be ready for several of the country's richest handicap races, probably in New York. Our reference to the heavy gold hanging from the finish wire is not unintentional, for the need of it is what brings back the Black for another try. As you know, Hopeful Farm lost its most valuable barn in a fire this week. It was not insured, and $100,000 is needed to replace the structure by next fall.

This kind of folding money may not seem very hard to get when Hopeful Farm has such a deadly racing duo as the Black and his three-year-old daughter, Black Minx, who is fresh from her great triumph in the Kentucky Derby. With the filly taking steady aim at the Preakness to be raced here next Saturday she may not need any financial assistance from her famous old man. But it looks as though the two magicians, Henry Dailey and Alec Ramsay, aren't taking any chances of their broodmares staying out in the cold this winter. They're brewing up another pot of that old black magic. We're glad to have been invited to dinner. Won't you join us?

Henry Dailey was the first to enter the railroad car at Pimlico and shortly thereafter he came down the ramp leading Hopeful Farm's stable pony, Napoleon. The Black seldom traveled anywhere without the old gelding and the photographers lifted their cameras to take pictures of him.

"Hold him still a minute, Henry," one called.

Napoleon stepped from the ramp with all the care and pride of a wealthy old gentleman being helped from his limousine by his chauffeur. He tugged a bit upon the lead shank, seeking more line so that he might raise his head still higher. He turned toward the cameras, his heavy ears pricked and very still. His round, butter-fat body was relaxed; his wise old eyes disclosed that he was well aware of what was going on and that he knew just how important he was as the Black's stable companion.

"Straighten up, Henry," another photographer called. "You're more sway-backed than he is."

"Naturally," the trainer answered. "I've been around a lot longer." Henry's bared head was whiter than Napoleon's coat and a lot thinner. He didn't smile at the remark that he'd made jokingly and he *did* make an effort to straighten up. It was getting more and more difficult to do that these days.

He was old, of course, but he didn't like to be reminded of it, Henry decided. The trouble with most people his age was that they kept thinking about how old they were and they never got anything done. His large, rugged hands gave a soft jerk to the lead shank. "Stop posing, you conceited old plug," he told Napoleon. "None of this is for you. In fact, just havin' your homely old face around again isn't going to help my morale any."

Napoleon lowered his big head and his ears wobbled and then fell forward as if from their own weight. Henry rubbed the gray's muzzle. "Forget it," he said apologetically. "I was just kiddin'. Besides, no one's payin' attention to us any more. They're lookin' at *him*."

The Black stood in the car's doorway, his great eyes brightening at the sound of repeated clicks of camera shutters and the calls from the crowd.

"Hold him up there a minute, Alec! Just a couple more."

"He ain't filled up in front at all," a horseman said, his voice raised so that all in his group could hear him.

"I told you he wouldn't be," another replied. "Didn't you hear Henry say that he's been out every day, running so much that they always worried about his being too *light* in flesh?"

"They sure don't have to take much off to have him ready to race," a jockey offered. "I heard Henry say that's the way he looked but I wouldn't believe it."

"If you ask me," a groom said, "he looks better than when I saw him in that Chicago race. Not so pretty maybe, but harder. Where'd he get those scars anyway? What kind of a place do they run up there at Hopeful Farm?"

"He didn't get them there," an exercise boy answered. "This horse gets around. He jus' don't stand up there at Hopeful Farm all the time."

"Yeah? What's he done besides bein' a sire?" the groom asked.

"You think all I got to do, Mac, is to tell you about the things this horse has done? *Don't you ever read?* Anyway, ain't it enough that you're *here,* watching the Black start his comeback in the big time again?"

"Sure," another groom agreed. "And what's the difference if he does look a little more ragged than he did before? Wind and speed is what y'need on the racetrack, not looks! Besides, for my money that's the way a horse should look! Turn 'em out, let 'em run, get 'em thin and hard! Let the fancy stock farms coddle their stallions and get those big filled-up fronts and weighted quarters. I'd sure like to be rubbin' this one, that's all I got to say!"

The black stallion, more than seventeen hands tall without looking it because his parts fitted together so well, moved to the top of the ramp. His great body, wet from his nervousness, caught the rays of the morning sun and reflected them. His small batlike ears flicked sideways, forward, then back while he listened to the boy beside him and the voices below.

Reporters noted the Black's mounting tension and watched him more closely, for in order to race, this great stallion must also be manageable. Speed without track manners was not good, and in earlier years the Black's natural instinct had been not to race but to do battle with those of his kind.

"Count" Cornwell watched and wrote the title "Horse Talk" on his scratch paper, knowing that it would be the subject of his column for the next day. He wasn't surprised by the Black's display of temperament. Long ago he had decided that there was a close relationship between the ability to win races and a high-strung disposition. A racehorse that needed constant reminding that man was master was one with a tremendous *will* to win as well as the physical capacity to win. If pressed, the columnist would admit that maybe his theory didn't always hold true, but he was certain it applied in this case.

Cornwell moved closer to the ramp, hoping to hear what Alec was saying to the Black. It would make a good column, this conversation between such a horse and his master. His *only* master, from all reports. No one else could do anything with the Black.

The Black raised a foreleg, bringing it down repeatedly upon the wooden ramp with dull, heavy thuds. Alec spoke to his horse but Cornwell couldn't catch the words. In fact he wasn't quite sure anything had been said. But the Black stopped his pawing.

Now the stallion was as quiet as the morning, standing proud and long limbed before the men gathered around the ramp. He did not move even when the camera shutters continued clicking incessantly and the photographers' cries of *"Just one more!"* shattered the still air.

Cornwell's eyes did not leave the horse. He knew no camera would ever catch the arrogance and nobility that were stamped on the Black's small, fine head. To be fully aware of these qualities in him one had to be here, standing close, watching the great eyes of the stallion as he looked down upon the people below. He might have been a king surveying his subjects. Suddenly the Black tossed his head and the silky foretop that crowned him dropped over his eyes. He half-reared and the arched crest of his neck became even more pronounced. It mounted high, then fell low, flowing powerfully into his shoulders.

Cornwell heard Alec Ramsay speak to his horse again. He listened quietly, paper and pencil ready. But in the end he wrote nothing. It was a language neither he nor his readers would understand, he decided. It belonged to Alec and the Black. Only occasionally had he heard an intelligible word. Most of it had been murmurings and touches, soft and gentle, and quick movements of the eye. Yet the Black had understood everything. Cornwell was certain of that. The columnist accepted this as an undeniable fact, but would his readers? Maybe he didn't have a column of "Horse Talk" after all.

"That's enough," Alec told the photographers. "I'm bringing him down now."

The Black came down the ramp a little too fast, a startled look in his eyes. The crowd fell back quickly but stopped moving when the stallion halted. The Black was listening to the sound of Alec's voice. He jerked his head high again and

held it still, all his senses keyed to the bidding of the boy beside him.

Henry Dailey said, "Come on, fellows. Open up now.
Give us a break. The show's over. You got your pictures."
Henry's bowlegs spun like a wheel as he hurried Napoleon
over to the Black's side. "Horses comin' through, fellows!
Make way!" he shouted.

Napoleon saw the crowd open up at their approach. He
snorted and enjoyed to the utmost his sense of usefulness. It
was good to be needed and wanted. He felt the Black's
weight as the stallion swerved sharply against him. Henry
patted him sympathetically but it wasn't necessary. He was
used to such bumps from the Black. It was his job to remain
patient and quiet while everything about him was a bedlam.

One of the reporters touched Henry Dailey on the shoulder as the small procession neared the long green-and-white
sheds. "How come you didn't let the Black finish out the
season at Hopeful Farm?" he asked.

"It seems we need a good handicap horse more than we
need another sire," Henry answered. "Satan's there."

"Then you think you can win again with the Black?"

"Sure. Why not?"

The reporter laughed. "Well, I can think of a lot of reasons but I'd rather listen to you. As far as I can remember
there was only one older horse that was ever able to come
back after being retired and that was Citation."

"That's your quote, not mine," Henry said. "I'm not worryin' about the Black bein' able to make a comeback, so
don't you worry, either."

They turned down one of the long shed rows and found
the Black's stall open and waiting for him. As Alec led his

horse inside, he heard another reporter say to Henry, "All this doesn't sound as though you have much confidence in Black Minx winning the Preakness next Saturday."

"What makes you think I haven't got much confidence in her?"

"Well, your need for a handicap horse like the Black *and* a hundred thousand dollars for that new barn."

"Nothin' to do with the Black," Henry said. "The filly will win us all the money we're going to need to build the barn."

Alec bent down to remove the Black's shipping bandages. The lower half of the door was closed and Henry was in the next stall with Napoleon.

"I'm told your filly didn't have much left after the Derby," Alec heard the same reporter remark.

Henry snorted. "You ever know a Derby winner who had?" he asked sarcastically.

"I only meant that a different winner could easily turn up in the Preakness."

"I suppose so," Henry snapped, coming around to the Black's stall door. "Why don't you wait and find out?"

Alec looked up from rolling the leg bandages.

"Now get this and that's all for today," Henry told the press. "We got the Black here to give him a crack at comin' back, and that's all he's here for. We're taking him up and trying him. It's as simple as that. If he doesn't come along or takes a lame step he's through and we ship him home fast. As you can see for yourselves we don't have to take much weight off him. He's been outside a lot and running. I got every confidence he'll race for us. But if he doesn't we haven't lost anything because we'd be here anyway with the filly. And we're not worryin' about the Black hurting himself in training because he could do that at home running in the fields. That's all I have to say. Now get on with you and let us get down to work."

Alec was rubbing the Black's legs when Henry finally entered the stall and knelt down beside him in the straw.

"Alec, why did you have to do it this way?" the trainer asked sadly. "He hasn't got a chance in the world of doin' us or himself any good!"

Again, the Derby

4

Alec stopped rubbing the Black's legs. "Why do you say that, Henry?" he asked. "Haven't you always wanted him to come back?"

"But not like this."

"Like what?"

"All the fanfare without a bit of preparation for his return," Henry answered. "The track handicappers will pack enough weight on him to stop a freight train. They'll mash him!"

Alec couldn't help smiling at Henry's outburst. He turned to the giant stallion who was pulling at the special clover hay Henry had got for him. "Such a poor, weak little horse," he kidded.

"It's no time to joke," the trainer flared.

"I'm sorry, Henry. I only meant that if we think he's the greatest horse in the world we must expect others to think so as well, and that includes track handicappers. After all, it's their job to equalize the field by weights, to give every horse in the race a chance to win." Alec turned to the Black again. "I don't think he'll break down under what they assign him in his races."

"Maybe not," Henry said gloomily, "but he won't win any races, either."

"We don't have to run him," Alec reminded the trainer. "If we think he's being given too much weight to carry, we'll keep him in the barn."

"That's exactly what I mean!" Henry said, stalking to the stall door. "What good will that do him or us? He might better be home."

Alec bit his lip in sudden anger. "How *did* you want it to be, Henry?" he asked.

"What good does it do now? He's here, isn't he? We can't send him back right away or it'd look like we were afraid."

"I'd still like to know," Alec said.

The trainer opened the stall door. "Sometimes in this business you can work a deal. He's a big gate attraction and I thought maybe they'd put less weight on his back if I took him to the West Coast. They go for big-name horses out there."

"So does New York," Alec said.

"Sure, but not at the expense of the race itself. They got a handicapper there who'd like to see every race end in a dead heat among the field. He'll pack the heaviest weight a horse has ever carried on the Black!"

Alec followed Henry out of the stall. He knew Henry could be right and it was one of the things he might have taken into consideration before announcing to the press that the Black was going back to the races. There was no avoiding New York, as their filly was due to run in the rich Belmont Stakes after the forthcoming Preakness.

Henry said with feigned lightness, "Don't look so glum, Alec. With the filly racing like she did in the Derby we've got a gold mine. She'll put up that barn fast all by her little self!"

Alec closed the screen on the upper half of the Black's stall door. It would keep out stray flies. Then he turned to the trainer. "I'd still like to enter him in some of the big New York handicaps just in case—" He stopped before the apprehensive look in Henry's eyes.

"Just in case the filly quits on us?" Henry asked. "Is that what you mean, Alec?"

The boy didn't answer fast enough and the trainer went on. "You're a strange fellow, sometimes. After the ride she gave you in the Derby I'd think you'd be so sold on her you could take off an' fly. Yet the last couple times you've worked her you've looked—"

Alec interrupted. "If she races as she did in the Derby I believe she'll be the first filly ever to win the Triple Crown."

"But you don't think she will. Is that it, Alec? When you worked her last week she loafed good, didn't she? An' that's what's troublin' you. You're forgettin' she loafed before the Derby too but I tricked her out of it. I can do the same thing again." Henry turned away angrily. "If you don't have confidence in her you oughta have it in me after all the years we've been together!"

"But I do!" Alec called at the trainer's back while Henry strode up the row.

Finally Alec turned to the stall on the other side of Napoleon. It wasn't really the filly's loafing through her works that bothered him. And it had nothing to do with her legs, her speed or her stamina. It was her eyes. They told him, just as if she'd spoken, that she was bored with racing, that anything after her glorious win in the Kentucky Derby would be an anti-climax. But how in the world could he have explained that to Henry?

He found Black Minx in a far corner of her stall, dozing. "Behave yourself now," he said softly, going inside. "Be a lady." She was quick with her hoofs, this one. It wouldn't do ever to try to surprise her. He put a hand on her; she barely opened her eyelids and then let them fall again.

Alec rubbed her smooth, short coat, which shone like glossy satin with the rays of the morning sun on it. Not a smudge of manure on her, not a bit of straw matted in her mane or tail, not a hair out of place. Just as slick, Alec decided, as when Henry had put her up last night. Here was gold that glistened as well as whinnied! Black Minx had the speed to go on to many other great victories if Henry could get it out of her. And the trainer believed he could do it.

"Open those eyes," Alec said, "so I'll know if Henry's right." But the filly kept them closed as if enjoying his soft touches to the utmost.

Black Minx looked small but she wasn't, for her appearance was very misleading. She had a lot more muscle than was noticeable at first glance. She was a big little girl, built to go a distance as well as for speed. But people generally weren't aware of that unless they looked her over very closely. That was why she had surprised so many of them with her performance in the Derby. Nobody had given her a second look until she'd been led into the winner's circle. Fillies weren't supposed to win the Kentucky Derby.

From now on the colts and their riders would be out to "get" her. She wouldn't have the advantage of taking them by surprise any longer.

Alec ran a hand across the strong, level back and down the shoulders that were deep and well sloped. Then he stooped over to take a look at the foreleg that had been injured at the start of the Derby. Black Minx had gone on to win with it and that had taken plenty of courage and determination. She was a daughter worthy of her great sire when she wanted to be! Fortunately the foreleg had healed nicely.

Then why didn't he share wholeheartedly Henry's confidence in her winning enough money for the new barn? Alec wondered. Was the look in her eyes all he had to offer by way of reply? Shouldn't he have more confidence in Henry's ability to get the filly to race? Henry had conquered all her earlier foolishness and she had gone on to win the Kentucky Derby.

Alec lightly pushed Black Minx's head away from him. "Keep them closed, then," he said. "It's better if I don't see them. Besides, you're only kidding yourself and me, too. Henry's the boss. You haven't got a chance of quitting on him."

When Alec left the filly's stall he saw two men carrying the Black's trunk from the railroad car into the tack room. Henry was just down the row talking to Don Conover, trainer of Wintertime. This horse had finished second to Black Minx in the Kentucky Derby. The two men were standing beside the colt's stall and Wintertime had his head over the half-door.

Alec looked in on the Black and found him still eating the clover hay. He went to the tack room and opened the trunk. The old saddle was in his hands when Henry entered the room.

"Kinda battered, isn't it?" the trainer asked, kneeling down beside the boy.

"Battle-worn, you mean," Alec answered, smiling.

Taking the saddle, Henry said, "It's seen plenty of battles, all right. I guess they'll let you ride with it."

"I wouldn't put anything else on the Black."

"It's been on a lot of famous horses, Alec. But it's a relic like me. It was my first saddle and when I started winning I was afraid to buy another, even though I could have afforded it."

"That's why I brought it along," Alec said. "We can use all the luck it'll bring."

Henry went to the door. "Let's put it on the filly and see how she works with it."

"What about walking the Black?"

"We'll do it later in the morning, when things quiet down around here." Henry paused, turning back. "And, Alec, get your silks. I want you to wear them."

"You mean *now?*"

"Yeah, put 'em on. I'll get the filly ready."

Alec stared at the empty doorway for several minutes before removing the all-black silks from the trunk. It wasn't his job to question orders and at the track Henry was a strict taskmaster, more trainer than friend. He'd find out soon enough what the old man was up to.

Pulling off his sweater, he wondered if Henry meant him to wear his jockey pants too. He decided he'd better do so, rather than take any chances of getting Henry started on one of his long tirades. He'd go all the way.

He put on his skin-tight white nylon pants and the long white cotton stockings, then he pulled on his high black boots. Standing up, he slipped on the black silk blouse and tucked the rich fabric into the top of his pants. He put on his black cap but left his goggles in the trunk; certainly there wouldn't be any need for them during his ride on the black filly.

He went to the door, stopped, and then retraced his steps to get something else from the trunk. When he left the tack room there were rubber bands around the wrists of his silks and he wore goggles over his black cap. He would have been dressed no differently on a race day.

Outside he stopped a moment, startled to see Wintertime over by the backstretch rail. Don Conover was at the colt's bridled head, waiting for the boy who came running across the track toward them. Alec recognized Billy Watts, and Billy too was wearing silks!

"What are you up to anyway?" Alec asked of Henry, who was adjusting the old saddle on Black Minx.

"I'm goin' to show you how I can get this lady to work," Henry answered.

"Is Wintertime part of it?"

Henry grunted in reply and then, taking Black Minx, he led her over to the occupied benches before the stables. Alec saw him remove his battered hat and give Jean Parshall, owner of Wintertime, his special smile for young ladies, particularly pretty ones. Alec didn't go any closer but he did listen to their conversation.

"I sure appreciate your letting Wintertime go along with us on this work, Miss Parshall," Henry said.

She laughed. "If it's all right with Don, it's all right with me, Henry. Although I honestly don't see why he wants to help you train the horse we're out to beat."

Henry chuckled. "Don wants a run for his money, I guess. We can't give it to him unless I can keep her in condition. She can't win on class alone, not over the Preakness distance."

Jean Parshall rose from the bench. "You had her ready for the Derby all right."

"I was lucky," Henry said, "and I had a good rider."

"*And* a good filly," Miss Parshall added.

"The best, when she wants to run or I can make her run."

"Temperamental?"

"Unpredictable, anyway." Henry smiled.

"Wouldn't you know it would be a filly?" she asked.

"I've known colts as bad," Henry answered.

"Horses are like humans. You must treat them no differently."

Henry straightened the filly's mane. "That's just what I'm about," he replied quietly.

Alec walked over to Billy Watts, who was about Alec's age and size. "What's going on?" he asked. "Are we racing the Derby all over again?"

"Could be." Billy smiled, pulling up the sleeves of his red silks. "Nobody's told me anything but I seem to be dressed for a race."

"So is Wintertime," Alec remarked.

Together they turned and looked at the colt's red-hooded head. The cup over his right eye was almost completely closed. Wintertime had had a tendency to run out, swerving to the right, before Don Conover had used the hood on him. Usually he wore it only on race days. He had learned that the hood meant business, so now he was moving sideways and on his toes.

Don Conover jiggled the bit to attract his colt's attention. Alec asked, "Are you still using a run-out bit on him too?"

"Yes, Alec," the trainer answered, "anything to keep him running straight. If he hadn't gone wide moving into the

Derby stretch we'd have caught you."

"I don't think so," Alec said. "We were meant to win that day."

Billy Watts's eyes were bright when he spoke up quickly. "We almost caught you, Alec. Another foot and we'd have made it." He pulled his red cap down hard on his big ears as if to lend added emphasis to his words.

Alec watched Wintertime. "Well, at least we both surprised the others who figured to win," he said. Wintertime was built much the same as Black Minx, strong and solid. Alec turned to his filly and found her looking at the blood bay colt. For long seconds he studied her eyes.

Don Conover spoke. "Yes, we surprised those big colts, all right. Not that I'm ever impressed by the height and heft of a horse. I always figure that a well-proportioned, good-muscled, medium-sized horse can beat the good big ones. They haven't got so much of their own weight to carry around with 'em, and there's not much difference in lung capacity."

Still looking at the filly and remembering her Derby race, Alec said, "And no difference at all in the size of their hearts."

"That's for sure," Don Conover echoed, but his eyes were only for his own colt.

Finally Henry led Black Minx over to them and she showed her aluminum-plated heels to the red colt. "Ready, Don?" Henry asked.

"We've been ready a long time," Conover said.

Henry chuckled. "I sure wish I had a pretty boss like you do."

Alec moved to the filly's side. "But you do, Henry," he

said, nodding in the direction of the filly.

Henry's face reddened while the others laughed at Alec's remark.

Don Conover said, "That saddle looks like you're down to your last dime. Where'd you get it?"

Henry grunted. "Never mind where I got it," he said. "But I wouldn't take any horse in your stable for it." He boosted Alec up and added, "Including Wintertime."

Don Conover grinned and Billy Watts nervously slapped his whip against his right boot. Wintertime jumped. Black Minx began to sweat. Alec took up rein.

Henry told Alec, "We're blowin' her out good. Three-quarters. Break her from the gate, and just hold on to the reins."

Alec saw Don Conover nod his head to Billy, who was now up on Wintertime. "Same thing," the trainer ordered, "only get out in front and stay there. Use your stick on him if you have to."

Henry said, "He'll have to use it plenty if you expect him to stay out in front."

Don Conover didn't answer.

Now Alec listened only to the filly. Her every movement told him that she would extend herself as she hadn't done since the Derby. She was trembling with eagerness to pull free of Henry's hand on her bridle. Her ears were pricked and her eyes were on Wintertime. It wasn't the first time she'd been worked with other horses but this was different. She must actually think it was race day!

Henry led her to the track behind Wintertime. Just up the backstretch the starting gate was being used by sets of horses. Alec leaned over, whispering in the filly's ear and trying to calm her down. But he felt the growing uneasiness in his own stomach. Wasn't the filly right in thinking she was going to race? Wasn't this to be the Kentucky Derby finish with Wintertime all over again?

Backside Backfire

5

When Black Minx's hoofs came down upon the track Henry turned her loose. She tossed her head and bolted.

"Easy now," Alec said. "We're in no hurry."

She swerved, trying to unseat him. He moved with her, his hands and knees firm, and got her straightened out again. He didn't mind her trying to get away from him. It settled his stomach. Now he could look at things the way they were. This was just a workout but Henry wanted the filly to think it was a race. Such strategy made him one of the finest colt trainers in the business.

The filly was excited now and that's the way Henry had planned it. She'd do no loafing this morning.

A set of four horses broke from the gate and came down the track toward them, their hoofs rocking the ground, their riders flashing whips and yelling. Black Minx nervously side-stepped but her eyes didn't leave the red-silked rider and colt just a few strides beyond.

Alec kept her from grabbing the bit. She tried to get it away from him by buck-jumping but he went with her, forward then backward in the creaking old saddle. He stood in the stirrup irons, catching his breath and wishing that Napoleon were alongside so he might use the gelding's big body as a buffer.

Billy Watts turned in his saddle. No longer was his face boyish but very grim and set, just as it had been before the start of the Kentucky Derby.

Alec's gaze met Billy's. It seemed that Black Minx wasn't the only one looking upon this as more than just a workout. He leaned sideways in his saddle, patting the filly's neck. He liked her eagerness but he didn't want her to go to pieces before they reached the gate. Her black body shifted uneasily and she reached for the bit again. Alec didn't let her grab it. There would be time for that in a minute or so.

The starter and his assistants were waiting for them, a little impatiently, Alec knew, for the starting-gate schooling hours were just about over. Yet the eyes of the men were filled with respect for the filly and colt who'd finished first and second in the Kentucky Derby.

Wintertime went behind the gate and the starter called from his platform, "What's this? A match race?"

One of his assistants laughed and answered, "It's a Derby Special, Hank."

"Better call it the *Preakness* Special," another joked.

Neither Billy Watts nor Alec said anything in return.

Alec waited until Wintertime went into one of the inside stalls and then he took Black Minx into the stall on the colt's right. Now nobody was talking or smiling. The starter watched while two of his assistants moved across the framework of the gate, helping with the horses. All was as it would have been in a race.

Black Minx went up, twisting in the close quarters of her narrow box. She came down against the padded sides without hurting herself.

"No chance. No chance," Alec called to the starter.

Black Minx's handler reached for her bridle to straighten her out and Alec said, "Other side, Kelly, please."

The man clambered to the right side of the stall. "Yeah, I remember now. She's been trained to be handled on the off side. Why? What d'ya want to be diff'rent than the others for?"

Alec didn't answer. Instead he kept the filly's head up. Small details helped win races and an assistant's holding a horse on the near side usually caused the horse to go off on the wrong lead and of course he'd go into the turn that way. Henry made certain his horses went off on the left lead so they'd go into the turn the same way.

The filly and colt were quiet. Alec took a deep breath. Through the wire-mesh door he saw the empty track. On his left Wintertime's red body was already shining with sweat. Black Minx, tossing her head, was just as wet. From the corner of his eye Alec saw the looming grandstand across the infield. Like the track, it too was empty. But for him and the filly, for Billy Watts and Wintertime, it was race day. In spite of what he'd told himself, this could not be considered an ordinary workout. He gave Black Minx the bit. "Okay, Baby, come out flying," he whispered. "Henry said to hold on to the reins and that's all I'm going to do."

The bell clanged and the front doors opened, freeing the two horses.

The filly and the colt broke from the gate together. Head and head, eye and eye, they pounded from the chute and into the long backstretch. There was no difference in their straining bodies or in the length of their strides. Nor was there any difference in the seats of their riders. Both sat very still and well balanced in their saddles, allowing their mounts to settle into racing stride without hurrying or worrying them.

Yet the colt and filly moved faster and faster, as if no force on earth could have stopped them. Black Minx was stretched out, hard against the bit, running the way she'd run in the Kentucky Derby. Wintertime's red-hooded head bobbed with hers. Neither had an inch over the other. Neither gave way.

They swept into the only turn with blinding speed, and the red colt edged out toward the filly. Then his rider used his whip just once and Wintertime stopped swerving and began hugging the rail again. Like the filly's, his strides were made for turns. But the red colt had the shorter way around, and going into the homestretch he was on top by a head's length.

Shouts rose from the great grandstand as white-coated cleaning men stopped their work to watch the very special race which was being run for them. But there were so few of them amidst the thousands of empty seats that their voices were lost in the sound of onrushing hoofs.

They saw the colt's rider start to use his whip again, moving it in rhythm to the strides of his mount without touching him. But the black filly wouldn't be left behind and once more drew even with him. Her jockey was still hand-riding but now his head and shoulders were moving, urging her on. She responded, slowly at first, then ever faster. She pushed her head in front of the colt's.

It was evident now that she was going on to win, even though she'd have to work for every inch. She surged forward, stretching out lower and ever faster. Relentlessly she came down the stretch, her head up and small ears pricked forward, her tail billowing like a cloak in her wake. She had less than a furlong to go to the finish line when suddenly her ears flicked to the right as if she were listening for something; then came a quick shifting of her bright eyes to the vast empty stands. She went on for another few strides, then suddenly slowed. The colt swept by her while she went the rest of the way in a very slow and easy gallop.

A little over an hour later Alec returned to the same section of track. The Black was with him, pulling a bit uneasily on the lead shank while his great eyes swept the towering grandstand.

"This is where she quit," Alec told him. "Henry said she was counting all the people who weren't there. He said he should have figured she'd do that."

The Black snorted and moved along the outer rail with Alec following.

After what had happened, Henry was convinced that the wearing of silks wouldn't be enough to fool the filly into working again even to the extent she'd gone that morning. But he wasn't giving up. Next time he planned to work her between races during the afternoon program. Then she'd have her cheering crowd.

The Black stopped to watch a tractor come around the first turn. He wasn't unduly excited by it, just interested, for he'd seen tractors pulling harrows at the farm.

The morning training hours were over and only by special

permission of the track superintendent had Alec been allowed to take the Black on his sightseeing tour around the sun-baked oval.

After the tractor and harrow had passed Alec said, "Let's get moving again so there won't be any travel kinks left in your legs."

It was quiet on the track compared to the stable area, but the Black had been manageable even there. Aside from a larger number of people, the activity in the stable area was not a great deal different from what he'd left at home. The Black was getting used to the loading and unloading of horses, the whinnies of mares, even the calls of other stallions. As at the farm the same trembling eagerness to go forward to meet them swept through his great body but he always awaited Alec's spoken command. Stable manners were as important as track manners, and Alec had worked hard on the Black.

Now the tall stallion stood still again, his eyes on the old clubhouse just off the first turn. For a moment he lifted his head high as though looking at the horse-and-jockey weather vane on top of the wooden frame building. Then he turned once more to the long, modern grandstand, whose freshly painted yellow-and-black boxes and thousands of other seats would be filled when the afternoon program began.

On Preakness Day there would barely be room to breathe and many more thousands of fans would spill into the infield to watch the running of the famous classic, the Run for the Black-eyed Susans. Would it be won by a black filly? It could, Alec decided, if she kept her mind on racing as she did for a while this morning. And she just might with such a crowd to cheer her on coming into the homestretch!

The Black tugged on the lead shank and Alec went with him.

"At least, if she goes like that she'll give a good account of herself," Alec said aloud. "We'd be proud of her—you and Henry and I. But nothing can be certain from now on. Just as *anything* can happen in the Kentucky Derby, *something* usually happens afterward to upset the winner from capturing the Preakness and the Belmont."

It was only a few hours later that Alec and Henry saw the "something" for that year come into view. They stood before a television set in a store across the street from the racetrack. Together they watched the running of the Withers Mile for three-year-olds in New York. They saw Eclipse, a burly brown horse with a white face, emerge from the tightly packed field and come billowing down the homestretch to set a new world's record.

Alec and Henry turned away, knowing Eclipse had come into his own and there'd be trouble ahead for everybody, including Black Minx at her very best.

"Bring on Eclipse!"

6

It wasn't often that a great horse came along as a three-year-old and when he did he presented a problem to everybody but those in his entourage. If he proved to be *truly* great, the number of horses in his age group who'd be sent out to race him would become fewer and fewer. No owner or trainer was likely to want his entry to take beating after beating. And when a situation like that developed, a track's most celebrated races could become nothing but "walkovers" for the champion, costing the management money and leaving the customers nothing to watch but a one-horse exhibition at a slow gallop.

It would be up to the trainers to decide if it was worthwhile having their three-year-olds race such a horse. The night following Eclipse's record-shattering victory in the Withers Mile the men at Pimlico were still unafraid.

Don Conover said, "One race doesn't make a horse *great*."

"We beat him in the Derby," Alec added confidently. "We can do it again."

Henry snorted. "He's not the same horse. He even *looked* different on the screen . . . bigger and higher in flesh."

"It's only been a few weeks since we last saw him," Conover scoffed. "He couldn't have grown much in that time. But you're right about one thing, Henry. He was long overdue for that kind of a race. I wish he'd put it off a little longer. Now we've got him right in our laps for the Preakness and the Belmont."

Alec banged a boot heel against the tack trunk on which he sat. "Don, this morning you said you'd take a good small horse any day in preference to a good big one."

"I still would," Conover reaffirmed.

Henry laughed. "Except for Eclipse, maybe?"

"No maybes," Conover answered.

"Henry," Alec said, "I think you're overestimating Eclipse. You've always liked him because he's burly and big. You like size. Don doesn't."

"That's right," Conover agreed. "I'm not scared of him at all. It's just that I know a problem horse when I see one."

Henry leaned back in his chair and surveyed the group in a bored way. "Y'got me all wrong, fellas. It's not that I have anything against a small horse. I like 'em *any* size, just as long as they can go. But the thing about Eclipse is that he's more than just big. There's nothing of the colt in him. There never was. He's all stallion and has been right along. As we know, a colt doesn't usually mature that fast. When he does, well, he's playin' with a bunch of kids and someone's goin' to get hurt."

A groom turned over a pail and sat down on it. He said,

"Eclipse was a big horse in the Derby but he sure didn't scare nobody. He got shoved around, too. It was just by luck he got up to be third."

Alec called to an exercise boy standing near the Black's stall. "Take your fingers away from that screen door or he'll mistake them for carrots."

"Better shut the top, Alec," Henry advised. "Let him get some sleep. Tomorrow will be a busy day."

"Okay, but I wanted him to get used to this."

"He will," Henry said. "You don't have to do it all in one day." He turned to the groom sitting on the pail. "You weren't watchin' Eclipse in the Derby or you would've known that they didn't push him around any. He fouled himself up. He's so big he got in his own way. That's been his trouble right along. But he got his legs straightened out today. I knew it would come. There was no stoppin' it. Just a matter of time."

Henry stood up. "That was a man-sized job he did today. Remember, it was Citation's world record that he broke. *Citation at five years old* on a fast California track! It's been in the books a long, long time."

"I'm impressed," Alec said. "But the chances are good that it'll be broken again."

"By a filly?" an exercise boy suggested.

A trainer leaning against Black Minx's stall door said, "She won't if she stops like she did this morning, Alec. She won't even get a chance to wave Eclipse good-by."

Henry moved down the row, stopped, and turned back. "She won't quit on us. Don't you worry none about that."

"I'm not worryin' none, Henry." The trainer laughed. "Are you forgettin' I have a colt goin' in the Preakness too?

Her stopping would suit me just fine . . . the earlier the better."

"She won't stop," Henry repeated angrily. "No filly's goin' to outsmart me."

Don Conover grinned. "Y'got a way with women, all right, Henry."

"You're not kiddin' none, Don. Now take your boss—"

"You'd better stick to two- and three-year-olds," Conover interrupted. "They're more your speed."

"I guess you're right," Henry answered soberly. "It takes some pretty smart thinkin' to handle 'em that young."

Another trainer grunted. "It's either that or they send you off to a madhouse."

"Tell 'em about that colt you picked up for almost nothin', Henry, because nobody wanted him," an old groom said.

Henry turned to him. "What colt's that?"

"You know . . . that gray one you had at Aqueduct. The one that'd quit in the stretch because he was so scared of grandstand noises."

"Oh, that one. He was just the opposite of the filly."

"Yeah, that one. He won for you 'cause you put earmuffs on him."

Henry grimaced. "Ear *plugs,* y'mean, not muffs."

"Sure, that's it. Tell 'em that story, Henry."

"You've already told it," Henry said, walking away.

"Where are you going?" Alec called.

"To bed," the trainer answered without turning back.

Don Conover called, "You're even gettin' to look like a horse, sleeping in that van of yours. Why don't you get a room? My landlady's got an extra one."

"I'll consider it now that Alec's here to keep an eye on the stable," Henry said, stopping.

"Sure," Alec encouraged, "go ahead."

"Not tonight. Maybe tomorrow," Henry answered.

"I'll believe it when I see you between sheets," Conover said.

Henry shuffled off toward Hopeful Farm's small black-and-white van. "Sheets and mattress don't make a bed," he said, his voice barely reaching them. "Any place but New York and I'm campin' out anyway. Might as well use the truck."

The groom sitting on the water pail laughed. "The big apple of his eye," he said. "Henry can hardly wait to get to Belmont!"

No one else spoke. The group broke up, most of them feeling no different from Henry. They were eager to return to the big track but first they had a race to run—the Preakness with a purse of more than one hundred thousand dollars.

Early the next morning Alec took the filly out to graze. It was Sunday and the racetrack was quiet except for the nickers of other grazing horses and the calls of their grooms.

As with everything else Black Minx was very particular in her choice of grass. She would stop to crop a few mouthfuls and then go on, trying to find another patch that was more appealing to her fancy and discriminating taste. But this morning she seemed to be constantly frustrated in her search and soon Alec found himself closer to the other horses than he cared to be.

"That's far enough," he said, giving the lead shank a tug. "We don't want to cause any trouble around here."

Black Minx stopped obediently but didn't graze. Instead

she held her head high, looking past the other horses without a flicker of interest.

Suddenly she gave a hard pull on the shank. Alec didn't let her go and, frustrated once more, she lowered her head to graze. After a few minutes Alec noticed that she was beginning to break out with sweat despite the coolness of the air. He took a large silk handkerchief from his pocket and rubbed her coal-black coat. Like a lady, she seemed to love the touch of silk, too. He had found that it pacified her more than anything else.

She's as hot-tempered as the Black, he thought. *Cross her in anything and she breaks out. Maybe it's true of all fast horses. No, Eclipse isn't like that at all. I've seen him galloped a couple of miles during the middle of the day with the temperature over a hundred and he didn't show a mark. In fact he didn't take more than a long breath or two.*

I wonder if he really is a great horse? Most of the guys seemed to think so last night. Ordinarily they won't go all out on a horse until he's been tried and proven over and over again. Even then they're awfully careful about calling a horse great.

Yet they're comparing Eclipse to Citation and Man o' War, even the Black! I don't understand it. Eclipse will have to prove to me that greatness isn't beyond him. Maybe he will—in the Preakness.

Suddenly Black Minx jerked up her head, her eyes bright and ears pricked. Alec noticed that her coat was becoming splotched with sweat marks again. Finally she kicked out hard, her flinty legs snapping the air.

Alec moved to her head, shortening the shank. The other horses—including Wintertime, who had just joined the group—were still grazing in the distance.

"Let's go in," Alec said.

Black Minx turned with him, sharply and willingly. Her hind legs split the air repeatedly and she came down on her toes. Alec pulled the shank to attract her attention. It wasn't unlike her to kick at another horse. But to be kicking when there wasn't the slightest chance of hitting her mark *was* strange. All the way back to the barn Alec watched her eyes, trying to figure out the coal-black filly.

Henry was waiting for them at the barn, the old saddle in his hands.

"Now we'll really get down to work," the trainer said. "Get the Black."

A few minutes later Alec was seated astride the great stallion, waiting for Henry and Napoleon to join them. There was no movement beneath him, yet he felt vibrations flowing between the Black and himself. With no other horse he'd ever ridden did he experience any such feeling.

Henry led Napoleon out of the stall and mounted. "All set?" he asked.

Alec nodded.

Henry prodded the gray gelding with his heel. "Come on, old horse," he said.

The Black swerved abruptly against Napoleon. Henry mumbled something after the crushing impact of the two bodies and moved his mount a little ahead of the stallion as they went to the track.

Henry had scheduled only a slow gallop for the Black. Even so, the press were waiting at the track gate for a look at the great horse. Photographers began pressing too close and Napoleon wheeled, lashing out with his hind legs.

The Black went along with him but didn't kick and Alec got him back in line. Now the frightened photographers kept their distance.

"Napoleon's a lot of horse this morning," Alec said quietly to Henry.

"What do you think a good stable pony's for if it isn't to keep order?" the trainer asked.

"Does that include our competition on race day?"

Henry grinned. "Let any horse get too close to him and he'll find out."

They rode onto the track. "Watch your horse," the trainer warned, "or he's liable to jump out from under you."

"I'm all right, but let go of us pretty soon."

"I will. I just want to keep Napoleon beside him another minute. Look at him breakin' out. Keep a tight hold, Alec. You're not goin' to gallop him with any twine string this morning. He'll want to take over. A mile gallop is enough for today. Don't let him get away from you. Take up on him. Watch him! Quick!"

The Black slammed into Napoleon but the old gelding withstood the blow, snorting a little and pushing back as was his job. He kept the stallion in line.

"I had no trouble at home," Alec said. "He's got plenty of miles behind him."

"This is the racetrack," Henry answered, as if that explained everything.

The trainer let them go at the head of the backstretch. Once free of Napoleon, the Black bolted. Alec allowed his horse to settle into stride and then pulled up on him, shortening rein and *asking* for obedience rather than demanding it. For several seconds there was no response. Greater became the stallion's strides and wilder the whip of his long mane and tail.

Alec longed to let the stallion go, to urge him on to his utmost speed. Instead he drew back still more on the reins.

Henry had said gallop, so gallop it must be. "Easy, Black," Alec told his horse. "Slow all the way down to a nice slow gallop. Not just a snug hold on you today but a tight one. Not even a breeze. That'll come later, maybe tomorrow. Maybe the next day. So will the fast works. It won't be long before Henry sets you down. Then you can go all out as you'd like to do. But now we've got to listen to him. Slower, still slower. That's the big guy."

Reluctantly the Black slowed, his ears flicking to the front, side and then back while he listened to Alec. He struck out playfully with his right foreleg and he never stopped asking for more rein.

Alec sat very still, watching the rail speed by and counting off the furlong poles. He belonged here as nowhere else in the world! His horse ran for the sheer love of running and he shared this love with him.

The Black rounded the far turn and went down the home-stretch, snorting at sight of the long, empty stands. He stretched out his head and dug in a little more but there was no release of the iron against the bars of his mouth.

"Easy," Alec repeated. "Not today. Easy. Easy. . . ."

The Black was listening to him, Alec knew. Otherwise there'd have been no holding him, bridle or not. His strides came slower and shorter. His oval-shaped hoofs beat on the track in quiet tempo. But there was nothing quiet within his great body. His eagerness to run was a living, breathing thing that constantly sought release. Alec felt the vibrations and they set him afire with a desire to let his horse go!

"Easy . . . easy," he began all over again, stilling temptation.

The Black finished the mile gallop and as Alec brought him to a stop he thought, *Why hasn't the filly inherited just a*

fraction of her sire's love for running? If she had, there'd be noth-
ing to fear from Eclipse in the coming Preakness. Instead she prefers
to romp and sulk.

But the following day between the third and fourth race
on Pimlico's afternoon program, Black Minx showed Alec
how wrong he was. Not only did the filly display the Black's
speed but his love for running as well! It just took a little
more prodding to get it out of her. In this case the stimulus
consisted of Pimlico's twenty-five-piece band, its members re-
splendent in their bright red coats; a grandstand and clubhouse holding that day some twenty-five thousand
screaming people; and last but by no means least the public-
address system that made known to one and all that they
were "looking upon the winner of the Kentucky Derby and
probably the fastest filly of our generation."

Black Minx went on to work the most sensational mile
and an eighth ever recorded at Pimlico racetrack. When she
had finished and her time was announced, the crowd applauded as they had done for no winner that day. Their uni-
fied call was, "Bring on Eclipse!"

Back in the stable area, Henry washed the filly and said,
"We'll have her sharp for the Preakness, Alec. She *loves* that
crowd."

"Any crowd," Alec corrected. "But you're right, Henry.
She'll be ready." He held the filly while Henry squeezed the
sponge over her head. Her long tongue came out, catching
the dripping water. Then suddenly she snorted, reared, and
came down on her toes. She lashed out with her hind legs,
sending the water pail flying.

Henry stepped back, grunting, but he wasn't angry with
her. Instead he chuckled and said, "She sure feels good, Alec.
That workout was just what she needed. But we mustn't

wind her too tight. She'll break like a watch if we do. Give her a little more line. That's it. Let her play around a bit."

Black Minx lifted her head, sniffing the wind; then she jumped forward, taking Alec with her. She rolled her eyes, showing the whites, but didn't fight him. Suddenly her eyes became intense and fiery. She moved quickly around Alec, her muscles showing strong and lean beneath her wet skin. Tossing her head she neighed, and then stood still.

Alec saw Wintertime being walked just a short distance away. Black Minx, watching him, again lashed out with her hoofs.

"I don't know what it is you have against him," Alec said, "but wait until Saturday and take it out on him then."

The filly snorted.

The Preakness

7

"Ladies and gentlemen," the race announcer said with grave dignity, "the horses are now coming onto the track for the running of the Preakness."

A respectful, almost reverent silence came over the great crowd. The members of the red-coated band rose to their feet before the stands and began to play. The spectators, too, stood up at the first strains of the immortal Preakness hymn.

"Oh, Maryland, my Maryland," many sang softly, their throats a little tight while they watched the horses coming out of the paddock gate.

Would Black Minx repeat her Derby triumph? Or would it be Eclipse today? How about Golden Vanity? And Wintertime— don't forget him! Maybe it would be Silver Jet. Or Olympus? Or the mudders, Lone Hope and Rampart?

Within the track's center field where thousands more watched the parading horses, an old gentleman removed his worn hat despite the light but steady drizzle. His lips moved as he drew himself up a little straighter, and his eyes were full.

To the tune of the Preakness Hymn he sang to himself in German, *"O Tannenbaum . . . Du grünst nicht nur zu Sommerszeit, Nein, auch im Winter, wenn es schneit. . . ."*

When the horses turned before the old clubhouse and came back in front of the grandstand, the band ended the hymn and broke into the rollicking strains of "Dixie!"

Now there were no more clogged throats or tear-filled eyes, nor was there reverent silence. Spectators called to horses and jockeys, while others sang at the top of their voices, "Oh, I wish I was in Dixie, away! Away! Away down south in Dixie. . . ."

The old gentleman in the infield had replaced his hat and was singing with those around him. And his eyes were bright with expectation as he said confidently to the stranger next to him, "It will be Wintertime today. He's a little horse but a very great one."

"Oh, no!" the stranger protested. "There's only one *great* horse in this race and that's Eclipse!"

The band stopped playing when the parading field reached the head of the homestretch and the announcer said, "Ladies and gentlemen, the horses are now in the hands of the official starter."

Alec took Black Minx far behind the starting gate. He expected Henry to leave but the trainer stayed alongside on Napoleon.

"Don't be nervous," Henry said. "We've got nothing to worry about. Her strides are suited for this kind of going. It'll be Eclipse who'll have trouble in the mud. Don't worry none. I don't need to tell you how to ride her. Use your own good judgment."

Napoleon lashed out with his hind legs at another stable pony who had come a little too close to Black Minx. The other pony kicked back and Alec let out the filly another notch, taking her still farther around the turn.

Henry continued talking, giving Alec many instructions despite his earlier orders to use his "own good judgment" in riding Black Minx.

Henry was the one, Alec knew, who was nervous and worried. The trainer was contradicting himself repeatedly and that wasn't like him at all.

"It's going to be all right, Alec. She's ready today," Henry said, keeping Napoleon close to the filly.

Alec didn't listen to Henry any longer. There was nothing anyone could do for him now. Like Black Minx, he was ready and eager to race. He just wanted to take his time going back to the starting gate. He didn't want to rush her. She was upset enough as it was. Let the others go to their starting stalls first and then he'd take her back.

He saw that he had almost reached the corner of Rogers Avenue and Old Pimlico Road. The wire-mesh fence was only a short distance away. He could see people standing on second-story porches of the houses across the street, watching him. Taxis and cars passed, their wheels sloshing the wet pavement. Black Minx watched everything that went on beyond the fence and Alec kept her attention there. There'd be time enough later for her to take in other things.

The light drizzle had stopped and the sun was beginning to break through the gray overcast. It wouldn't make any difference in the condition of the track, Alec knew. After last night's heavy rain, the strip was heavy and holding.

Alec heard the starter's metallic voice through the amplifier calling him. "Bring your horse back, Ramsay."

Turning the filly around, he saw that the other horses were making their way toward the gate. None of them seemed to be in any hurry, though. Henry, still alongside, was silent. Alec turned the filly's head toward the infield so that she could watch the crowd there.

The sun's reappearance would make the afternoon a lot more pleasant for all those people, he thought. They were very quiet compared to the Kentucky Derby fans and their eyes were only for the horses. There were no loud catcalls to jockeys, no frantic rushing and shoving for a better view of the start. Instead they talked softly while craning their heads a little higher to watch the field go to the post. It was a good crowd, a polite crowd who knew horses and had come to watch a horse race . . . not one another or a sideshow. It made sense to Alec, horse sense.

As the field neared the starting gate, Henry left him.

"She's all yours, Alec," the trainer said with final simplicity. "Good luck."

Alec let Black Minx move a little faster and her strides were secure in the mud. She was a fastidious little filly who preferred not to get her feet wet or dirty, but she had no fear of slipping . . . and that was all-important today.

Her eyes were on the other horses now and, of course, she knew what it was all about. She had worked well and as Henry had said, "It's going to be all right. She's ready today."

Alec smiled. She had her crowd. Not as big as the Derby one, perhaps, but her second biggest; all that was necessary to make her go the race of her young life. She'd better!

Alec knew that it wasn't going to be a two-horse race as a lot of people figured. It would not be simply a duel between Eclipse and Black Minx. Every horse in the race bore watching just as in the Kentucky Derby.

He watched Golden Vanity go into his number 1 stall.
The California champion had quit during the last furlong of
the Derby. But might not this shorter distance of a mile and
three-sixteenths be just right for him?

Black Minx suddenly broke from Alec's hands, bolting
away from the outer rail where he'd been keeping her. He
stopped her just before she reached the starting gate but not
in time to keep her from lashing out with her hind legs and
narrowly missing Wintertime.

Billy Watts on Wintertime swung his stick at Black
Minx, and the starter from atop his high platform just off
the track said, "Take your filly back, Ramsay, or I'll put you
outside. Smith," he called to one of his ground crew, "you'd
better help him get her straightened out. We don't want any
trouble here."

The crewman took Black Minx's bridle, leading her across
the track toward her number 5 stall.

Alec stroked the filly's neck and talked to her, but he
couldn't understand her hostility toward Wintertime. The
only explanation he could think of was the humiliating defeat Wintertime had given her in their one workout together. But she had quit of her own accord, so that didn't
make much sense. Alec didn't have time for any further
thought on the subject for Silver Jet reared, refusing to be
led by his handler, and came down close to the filly.

The gray's handler got hold of the bridle again and coaxed
him into the number 2 stall.

Silver Jet and Golden Vanity were now side by side!
Would the two of them set the same blistering pace they
had in the Derby? Alec wondered.

Wintertime went nervously into the next stall, number 3,

and Black Minx watched him, snorting loudly. Alec patted
her again.

"Come on, Girlie," her handler said, "that's no way for a
Kentucky Derby winner to act." The man tried to get her to
move toward her number 5 stall but she wouldn't budge.

Alec said, "Give her another minute, please. Don't fight
her."

"We ain't got another minute," the crewman said. "It's
post time now. But I'll give her another couple seconds."

Burly brown Eclipse went into the number 4 stall as if he
were going into his barn for a container of oats.

"That's the way he does everything," Alec recalled. "It's as
though he knew exactly how much work had to be done in
order to earn his keep!"

It wasn't that Eclipse was sluggish. Far from that. Rather,
he seemed to know how to relax completely, to bide his time
until the very second the gate doors opened and the race was
on. Now, standing quietly in his stall, his head with the
white blaze seemed actually to droop. Unlike most of the
others, including Black Minx, there wasn't a spot of perspiration on his big body.

The crewman suddenly had Black Minx going forward
and she didn't fight him. Into the number 5 stall she went,
standing still while the crewman climbed noisily about the
framework of the gate. It was as if she knew the time had
come for all foolishness to end.

"Other side, Smith, please," Alec said quietly. "She han-
dles from the off side."

"Yeah, I know," the man said, moving over.

Alec looked to his left and found Ted Robinson surveying
him from atop Eclipse. "You seem to have grown," Alec
said lightly.

"Funny, but he does seem to get bigger every time I ride him," Robinson answered, smiling.

"Today we cut him down to size."

"No, Alec," Robinson said with abrupt soberness. "I've been up on a lot of them. This one is the best. He's the best there ever was."

The doors slammed shut in the next stall, frightening Black Minx. She tried to rear but Alec kept her down. He didn't turn again to Ted Robinson. He knew that while Robinson wasn't any older than he, Ted had more years of riding behind him. If Robinson, too, hailed Eclipse as a true wonder horse, it was going to be a tough job beating him.

The crewmen had Olympus in the stall to Alec's right now, number 6. The last two horses, Lone Hope and Rampart, weren't giving their handlers any trouble. They were going inside.

Alec talked to his filly. Any second now and they'd be off. He felt her reach for the bit. He kept it from her but let her play with it so she'd have something to do.

Far down the homestretch and on top of the ancient cupola of the clubhouse he noticed that the horse-and-jockey weather vane had turned to the west, promising good weather for the rest of the afternoon. The next day, he knew, the jockey's colors would be repainted to match those of today's Preakness winner. Would they be the black-and-white of Hopeful Farm? Or Eclipse's maroon-and-white? Or Silver Jet's black-and-crimson? Or Wintertime's . . .

Alec heard the last stall door slam shut and focused his eyes on the stretch of lonely road directly before him.

It was a muddy, sloppy track. Black Minx would take kindly to it but she wouldn't relish it. Too bad Pimlico didn't work more sand into the loam so that horses would find the going secure even when the strip was drenched. That's the way it was at Belmont.

Golden Vanity reared high in his stall and Nino Nella, his jockey, called to the starter, "No chance! No chance, sir!"

"Don't worry," the starter answered. "We'll wait. We've got lots of time. Don't get your horse and the others all excited now, Nella. Nice and easy does it. Plenty of time. Don't worry."

Olympus, on one side of Alec, threw himself against the padded sides. Eclipse, on the other side, raised his head and waited patiently. Black Minx fidgeted.

Alec noted that the track was now completely in shadow from the stands. It was getting late. They should have been off minutes ago. Rampart snorted and backed out of his stall to complicate matters still more for the starter. The filly shook her head.

"Easy, Baby," Alec said. "Just a few seconds now."

The spectators on either side of the track were very quiet. Some of those in the center field had climbed atop the steeplechase barriers to get a better view. The water jump in front of the grandstand was full and overflowing. Alec remembered other days when it had been so hot that there'd been no water at all. But not today, no sir.

The track had been cut up from previous races and muddy water filled the depressions made by many hoofs. Near the inside rail was an untouched path about four feet wide. Jockeys kept off the rail in wet going, for as a rule the mud was deeper there.

Alec's eyes remained on the unmarked inner lane. If this track was well graded the going there might not be as bad as jockeys in previous races had thought. He wondered if the

Preakness riders would stay off the inside too. If so, he just might try . . .

The bell rang, the front doors slammed open and the horses broke from their stalls. The Preakness was on!

Black-Eyed Susans

8

Black Minx grabbed for the bit, but Alec kept it from her. He wanted to be able to help her in case she slipped before settling into stride. She wobbled when she was a few feet away from the gate but he got her out of it. On their left Eclipse skittered as though sliding on ice and almost went down, his legs flaying wildly. Black Minx pulled away from him.

Maybe Henry was right, Alec thought. Maybe they wouldn't have to worry about the big horse today after all!

Mud and dirty water splattered all around Alec but did not hit his face. Not yet. It wouldn't at all if no horse got in front of them. Alec didn't urge the filly to go faster. He wanted her to settle into stride first.

"No hurry," he called softly. "No hurry. Take your time."

Mud suddenly began flying at his goggles, filling them so he could hardly see. Now he was getting it. From whom? It wasn't Olympus. Olympus was coming in on his right and sliding!

Alec yelled at Olympus's jockey and had to climb all over Black Minx, trying to get a hold on her to keep from going down. Suddenly the filly jumped ahead, her hoofs for the first time secure in the sloppy footing. They pulled clear of Olympus but the mud kept coming at them from in front.

Alec saw that it was Rampart and Lone Hope who had crossed ahead of them. Racing from the far outside, the two colts went to the lead and swept under the finish wire for the first time with a mile still to go! Just behind them raced Wintertime and then came Golden Vanity and Silver Jet both under a snug hold and to the filly's left. The last two colts were going to be kept off the pace this time, Alec decided. Their riders were letting Rampart and Lone Hope go to the front, content to make their bids later in the race.

Alec heard a tremendous roar from the stands and wondered if anything had happened to Eclipse. The burly horse had been having so much trouble that he might have gone down!

Black Minx hated the mud flying in her face. She shook her head and tried to avoid it. Alec took her a little more to the right of the front runners as they swept into the turn at the old clubhouse. They were all staying away from the rail, he saw. But he didn't want to take Black Minx over there yet. It was too early to make his bid. Like most of the others he was rating his mount, saving her for the grueling run down the long backstretch and then around the far turn headed for home!

The field had straggled out but the positions remained unchanged. Rampart and Lone Hope were still running as a team and had increased their lead to three lengths. They had a lot of early speed in this mud but Alec was certain they didn't have the stamina to keep it up.

Wintertime was next and running a little to the leaders' right. He was going under wraps, his strides like the filly's coming effortlessly and very secure. He was in an excellent position to take the lead without much trouble. Alec decided he'd be the colt to beat if Eclipse was already out of the running.

He took Black Minx a little higher on the turn, ready to let her out a notch going down the backstretch.

Golden Vanity and Silver Jet were directly behind the two leaders, saving ground. Their jockeys were sitting quietly in their saddles. It wouldn't be long now before they'd make their moves. They'd make it hot for Wintertime up there!

Alec tagged along, content to stay where he was for the time being and confident that his filly was ready for the task which lay ahead of them. She was eager to go on and the others were being so cooperative by staying off the rail!

The leaders increased their pace going into the backstretch and Alec let Black Minx move along faster with them. It still wasn't time for him to make his bid. Alec listened for the flat, sucking sound of hoofs behind him. He knew what was in front and what he had to do. It was what might be behind him that bothered him a little. He didn't want a horse suddenly coming up to botch things for him. Eclipse and Olympus were there, somewhere. Or were they? He couldn't hear them so maybe they'd gone down when that roar had come from the stands early in the race. He didn't want to look back to find out. Too many races had been lost by riders doing just that. Anyway he was about ready to make his move.

"Listen to what I'm telling you," he said aloud and in time to the filly's strides. "You're full of run, full of run. Oh, Preakness, here we come, here we come. . . ." He let her take the bit and guided her over toward the inside rail. "Here we come. . . ."

The horses had passed the middle of the backstretch, and with a half-mile to go their moves began! Wintertime swept up, passing the two sprinters in front, and took the lead. Nino Nella, riding Golden Vanity, rocked wildly in his saddle as his mount moved up with Wintertime. A stride to their rear came Silver Jet with his jockey sitting still in his saddle but showing the gray colt the whip without touching him.

Alec watched Lone Hope and Rampart dropping back. They were spent and through. All he had to do was to avoid them and go on. He took up on the filly again, ready to catch her if she wobbled in the new, untouched footing; then he sent her over to the rail.

There was no hesitancy in her strides as she swept onto the inner path. Nor did she slip. In fact her hoofs came down even more securely than before. The mud was no deeper on the rail than anywhere else!

Sighting between her small ears, Alec aimed for the clear, unmarked road before them. He let Black Minx have the bit again and she surged forward, passing Lone Hope and Rampart on the *inside*. He saw the surprise on the faces of the jockeys as he took Black Minx past them.

"Three more to go!" he called to her. "And it's all clear sailing! Here we come . . . here we come!"

The shouts of horsemen standing on stable roofs just off the backstretch reached him. Their calls were for Black Minx as she went up on the rail. The jockeys in front didn't know she was on her way. They wouldn't know until she swept through the inner lane they'd so politely left open for her!

Black Minx caught Silver Jet and Golden Vanity going into the far turn. Their riders were barely aware she was alongside before she'd gone on! Then all they could do was to move over to the rail themselves to save ground and close a gap that already had been used by a black filly. They began working feverishly with hand, heel and whip to wring every last ounce of speed out of their mounts.

Black Minx was going all out and Alec made no attempt to hold her back. He was confident she had the stamina to stay until the very end of this race for the black-eyed Susans!

Wintertime was two lengths beyond her and still keeping well off the rail. Billy Watts used his whip once as his colt started to climb even more to the right on the banked turn. Under the sting of the whip Wintertime straightened out and swept into the homestretch. Billy Watts tapped him again to keep the colt's mind on his business, for he'd heard the sudden rush of oncoming hoofs. He didn't look behind to find out who it was.

Alec saw the nervous twitching of the filly's ears as she drew up on Wintertime. He gave the bit a hard yank to keep her attention away from the colt and on the open path before them. He didn't want any trouble now with the race within their grasp.

Suddenly from the great stands rose the mightiest roar Alec had ever heard on a track. At that precise second Black Minx caught Wintertime and Alec thought the applause was for her!

"Go on!" he called softly. "They're shouting for you. That's what you wanted to hear. Listen to them!"

She didn't respond. For a second Alec thought it was because Wintertime's speed had quickened under Billy Watts's constant urging. But it *hadn't,* for out of the corner of his eye he could see Golden Vanity moving up on a *tiring Wintertime*!

Alec began moving in his saddle, urging Black Minx on as he'd done in the Kentucky Derby stretch. She had responded nobly then, but now she refused his demands even though she had the speed and stamina for them. Golden Vanity drew alongside Wintertime and then went to the lead. Black Minx bobbed head to head with Wintertime, neither gaining on nor losing ground to the red colt. As a team of equal size and stride they went into the last furlong of the race a length behind Golden Vanity.

The pandemonium on either side of the track rose to still greater heights. It was only then that Alec realized that even before, when Black Minx had caught Wintertime, the loud clamor had not been for them. *It had been for Eclipse, coming now on the far outside of the track!* The big horse passed them and then swept by Golden Vanity with electrifying speed; he pulled farther and farther away, winning by a dozen or more lengths. Behind him finished Golden Vanity and in a dead heat for third place came Wintertime and Black Minx, still head to head.

Later the crowd was so dense around Barn J that there was no place to cool out a horse. After washing Black Minx, Alec and Henry took her away from the throng gathered there to idolize Eclipse.

Henry pulled the filly's black-and-white cooler higher up on her head, pinning it securely around her neck. "Well," he said resignedly, nodding toward the photographers, "that was us at the Derby."

Alec said, "She could have done it again."

"I don't know," Henry answered. "I'm inclined to doubt it. Eclipse came off that fast pace with an explosive burst of speed that I've seen equaled only by the Black. You know it was the track record he broke as well as the Preakness record, don't you? On that kind of a track, too!"

"I know," Alec said, "but I still think that if she'd kept going—"

Henry interrupted, "Maybe. Maybe so. She had a good lead on him comin' into the stretch. At least it would have been something to see!"

The trainer's eyes left Alec for the filly and then he walked on in silence. Finally he said, "Well, we made something today, over eleven thousand dollars. And no one's countin' us out of the Belmont. We'll get that barn built yet."

They joined the other horses and men in a walking ring far from the crowd. Suddenly the filly was on her toes, her small hoofs barely touching the ground before she had them up again.

Henry gave a tug on the lead shank to keep her still. "Easy, Baby," he said. Then turning to Alec he added, "Don't think for a minute I won't figure out why she didn't go to the front this afternoon. I'll fix her, all right. No horse is goin' to outtrick me."

Alec was silent when Henry had finished. His eyes left the filly and centered on Wintertime, who was on the opposite side of the ring. After another moment or two he said, "I don't believe you'll be able to do anything about this, Henry."

"Don't be silly, Alec," the trainer replied irritably. "There's nothin' I can't do something about. What makes you say that, anyway? What do you think is wrong with her?"

"Well . . ." Alec began. Then he stopped and started over again. "There's nothing really wrong with her."

"There's got to be," Henry retorted. "It's not right that she didn't go on to make a race of it with Eclipse, is there?"

"No, but—"

"Speak up, Alec!" Henry said in exasperation. "Don't fuddle so."

"You'll think I'm awfully silly, Henry, but I'm sure it's—" Alec turned his head away from the impatient trainer. "I'm sure she's in love with Wintertime," he went on sheepishly. "That's the reason she wouldn't go by once she'd caught up with him." He got the last sentence out as quickly as he could. The rest was up to Henry.

The old trainer's jaw dropped. He saw that Alec wasn't fooling. *"Oh, no,"* he said.

Futurity Farm?

9

Shortly after four o'clock the next morning Black Minx and her famous sire were on their way to Belmont Park in the small van. They stood straight in their stalls separated by Napoleon, their legs bandaged to protect them from the rigors of travel.

Alec watched them through the cab window while Henry drove. He didn't expect any trouble even though Black Minx had reared and bucked on her way to being loaded. Maybe she had just felt good. Or she might have figured she was leaving for the farm and didn't want to go.

"That's more like it," he said aloud. "She probably thought she was leaving Wintertime for good."

"What's that?" Henry asked sleepily without taking his eyes from the road.

"I was figuring that she buck-jumped back there because she didn't want to leave her boy friend behind."

Henry snorted. "Didn't you tell her that he was getting ready to leave for Belmont, too?" he asked sarcastically. "You've been talking pretty silly since yesterday, Alec. No sense stopping now."

Alec put the equine first-aid kit in the compartment behind his seat and then said, "You asked me what I thought and I told you. It's as simple as that. I'm not saying I'm right. You asked me, that's all."

"Don't get sore," Henry said. "Anyway it's too early for that kind of heavy thinking. Why don't you get some more sleep?"

Alec didn't answer and he didn't close his eyes. It wasn't that he didn't trust Henry's driving but they were carrying very valuable cargo and he wanted to be alert.

The Baltimore streets were empty and the night air was very cool. It made for easy and pleasant going. Down Rogers Avenue they went and into Belvedere, then by the park to York Road before they turned north to Towson, Maryland. From there they went east until finally they sped along U.S. Route 1. Ahead were the lights of other horse vans and behind them rolled the rubber wheels of many more. The trek to Belmont Park was on!

Alec broke the silence in the cab by saying, "After yesterday I guess even the more cautious among the horsemen will be calling Eclipse 'great,' won't they?"

"Does that include you, Alec?" Henry asked.

"I don't think I'm any judge. It's necessary to have been around a long time to decide."

"Like me, y'mean?" Henry asked, grinning. "Old and tottering?"

"Yes, like you," Alec agreed seriously. "For instance,

while I know Eclipse has broken a world's record and a track
record in his last two races I still don't know if that makes
him a 'great' horse."

"You're right there," Henry said. "Comparin' Eclipse's
times with those we know as truly great horses doesn't mean
too much. In the old days the tracks weren't as fast as they
are now. Also, some of the most famous horses weren't even
extended in their races so we don't know what their best
times would have been. But if you've *seen* them in action
you're able to form some kind of opinion as to how Eclipse
compares with 'em."

He stopped the van before a small town's traffic light and
waited for it to change before saying with sober deliberation,
"I saw such 'greats' as Sysonby and Colin and Man o' War. I
believe that Eclipse, as far as he's gone, is the equal of them
and others."

For long moments Alec was silent. He weighed Henry's
words over and over again, realizing that the trainer believed
whole-heartedly in Eclipse's greatness. Finally he said, "I still
think the filly can beat him."

Henry shook his head. "I don't believe any three-year-old's
goin' to beat him, Alec. Nor even the best of the older
horses, if they happen to meet. Except, perhaps—" He
stopped.

"The Black?" Alec put in.

"Well, frankly, I wasn't thinkin' of him," Henry answered. "I hadn't figured on their meetin'. But take Casey.
He just might race Eclipse before the year's over."

Alec nodded. Casey, a chestnut gelding by Bold Irishman
out of Swat, was the darling of the New York tracks. He had
shown no early speed and had done nothing of consequence
as a two- or three-year-old. But at four he began picking up

horses fast and had won several big handicap races. This year, at five, he had not lost a race although he'd campaigned heavily in Florida as well as New York.

"Yes," Alec said, "Casey's a lot of horse. I hear they're already calling him the year's handicap champion."

"They better after the way he won yesterday in New York," Henry said.

"What race was it?" Alec wanted to know.

"The Metropolitan Mile. He equaled the world's record Eclipse set last week in the Withers."

"Carrying how much weight?" Alec asked incredulously.

"One hundred and thirty pounds."

"Four pounds more than Eclipse had on his back," Alec said thoughtfully.

"And over the same track," Henry reminded him. "Belmont."

Alec stopped watching the cars ahead and turned to Henry. "Only a few minutes ago you said comparative times were of little value in judging horses," he challenged.

"That's when some fifty years or more separate the two," Henry corrected. "No, Alec, Casey's time deserves a lot of attention."

Alec's gaze was once more on the road. "You'd better call him 'great' too if you're pinning that label on Eclipse."

"Perhaps so," Henry said cautiously. "I want to see him go first."

"Since we'll all be at Belmont you'll get your chance."

"Nice and cozy," Henry replied, turning off the van's headlights. It was now light enough to see without them.

They rode for many minutes in thoughtful silence and then Henry muttered more to himself than to Alec, "If I could just tighten up on him . . ." He stopped and turned to Alec, finding the boy's eyes searching his. "The Black, I mean. I want him ready. No one seems to be foolin' around these days. Not the way the records are goin'."

"He galloped well all last week," Alec pointed out.

"I know," Henry agreed, "but a race would do him more good than a month of gallops and works. The only trouble is they'll pack so much weight on him he'll hardly be able to move. I can't see that kind of a race doin' him any good."

"Why don't you try him and see? They might not assign him as much weight as you think."

"I believe I will—since you've suggested it, that is."

"When?" Alec asked, knowing Henry had planned this race for the Black all along.

"In the Speed Handicap. It's only seven furlongs, not long enough to hurt him even if he's carryin' a lotta weight."

"This week?" Alec asked thoughtfully.

"Wednesday," Henry answered.

Alec didn't say any more. He couldn't. His throat was tight as it was at the mere thought of going postward with the Black *so soon*!

Four hours later Alec and Henry went through the Holland Tunnel and then moved slowly across lower New York to the East Side. It was there that Henry suggested using the Queensborough Bridge to reach Long Island so they'd pass through their old neighborhood in Flushing, where they'd first met.

"I haven't been back," Henry said. "How about you?"

"Just once," Alec answered. "It's changed a lot. I'd rather remember it the way it was."

"It won't do any harm for me to see the changes," Henry said with sudden bitterness. "I've seen plenty of 'em in my time. One more won't hurt."

Alec looked at his friend and in the glare of the morning sun he noticed for the first time how tired Henry looked. Well, Alec decided, he probably didn't look very fresh himself, having been up since three o'clock. He turned to the rear window of the cab and watched the Black play with the flat board they'd put in his water tub to keep it from splashing. Napoleon and Black Minx were dozing. They were good travelers.

Alec thoughtfully studied Henry's face again. Even allowing for their early rising, his friend's expression was much too grim, his eyes too sad. Why? It was more than plain, ordinary tiredness. Was just the prospect of seeing his old home again responsible? In spite of his mockery of all the changes he'd seen during his life?

An hour later they went down Flushing's Main Street and past the Public Library. After a few blocks more they approached a small open field where the Black had first grazed. It was occupied now by parked cars, hundreds of them, it seemed.

Henry stopped the van within the tall shadows of newly built apartment buildings and surveyed the breaks in the old stone fence through which the cars had been driven. "Since I still own this land all I gotta do is start chargin' for auto storage and we could build the new barn," he said harshly.

"It's close to the subway station," was all Alec could think of to say. "And no one's here to keep them out."

Henry threw the van into gear and drove up the driveway to the tightly shuttered two-story frame building. Here, too, were parked the cars of subway commuters to New York City.

"Welcome home," Henry said, getting out of the van.

Alec got out too. Henry didn't go into the house but

looked at it for a long time. Then he walked around to the back, Alec following. Together they stood in front of the ivy-covered barn. Neither suggested going inside to look at the Black's old stall. After a few minutes they went back to the van.

"I could sell this place," Henry suggested. "It's pretty valuable with all the apartment buildin' goin' on."

"I wouldn't let you do it," Alec said firmly.

"Why not?"

"You know why. It means a lot to us. It's where it all began. Someday we'll have the money to fix it up and keep it that way."

"There's no reason to," Henry said despondently. "All that you're talking about is done. Gone like Clara—"

Henry stopped after mentioning his dead wife's name and Alec let him alone. The van pulled out into the heavy traffic again.

After a long while Alec said, "Just the same, someday we'll know the right thing to do with it."

Henry wiped his nose. "Hangin' on to old places and memories only weighs a guy down," he said. "I'm slowin' up enough as it is."

"Don't be silly, Henry."

"Don't *silly* me," the trainer returned in sudden anger. "I know what I'm talkin' about. Men my age aren't worth anything. We just like to *think* we're necessary. We like to kid ourselves along."

Alec didn't say anything in the face of Henry's fury. He kept watching the traffic while Henry maneuvered the van with steady and skillful hands. He knew, of course, that revisiting the old home was responsible for his friend's depression. He realized, too, that the mood wouldn't last long.

No longer than his angry tirades did when he was getting a horse ready to race. The only thing to do was to keep quiet and agree with him if he asked for an opinion. Later on it could all be straightened out.

"Old men have got no place in this business," Henry went on tiredly. "We look back too much instead of ahead. Always talkin' about the way it was. What's the past worth anyway? *Nothin'!*" he bellowed. "It's the future that's important. Keep your eyes always ahead of you. That's what you've got to do!" He turned abruptly to Alec, his keen gaze seeking the boy's reaction to his theory.

"Sure. Sure," Alec answered agreeably.

"You're darn right I'm right!" Henry said, his gaze returning quickly to the road. "That's why I've thought all along that a better name for our place would be Futurity Farm! It's you and the young stock that's goin' to make us or break us. Old-timers like me are just along for the ride!"

"Sure," Alec said again. Anything to keep Henry happy.

"Y'mean you don't mind?"

"Don't mind what?" Alec asked.

"Changin' our name to Futurity Farm! Haven't you been listening to me?"

"Yes, I've been listening. Futurity Farm it is then, if that's the way you want it," Alec answered hurriedly. But inwardly he was asking, *What about the other old-timer in the back, Henry? Aren't you forgetting that if it wasn't for him and you there'd be no farm to name, no present or future? But call us Futurity Farm if you like. Or anything else for that matter. It's what's behind the name that's important—just as important as what's ahead. But I'm not going to say that, not now.*

Henry was silent for the next fifteen minutes, but there was no softening of the grim outline of his face. Alec began to wonder if this was more than just one of Henry's temporary moods. He was about to break the silence when suddenly Henry's face lit up.

"Say, there's a friend of mine!" he shouted. "Mike! Michael Costello!" Henry brought the van to a halt at a corner bus stop. "Mike," he called again through the open window on Alec's side. "It's me, Henry Dailey!"

There was a large group waiting for the bus and Alec had no idea which of the men was Henry's friend until a small, wiry man emerged from the throng and, hopping onto the running board, opened the door. Alec moved over, making room for him on the seat.

"Is it offerin' me a ride ye are, Henry Dailey?" the man asked in a soft Irish brogue.

Henry slapped the man on the shoulder before starting the van. " 'Tis the truth ye speak," he said, mimicking the other's accent. "Ye didn't fool me, old boy, with that yellow-bowled pipe in your mouth and that gay-lookin' cap on your head." Henry swept off the man's cap, exposing a shiny, hairless skull.

"Cover me head!" cried the man sharply, grabbing for his cap.

Henry chuckled and returned the cap. "Now I'm sure it's you, Mike," he said in his normal voice. "Alec, meet the man who back in my ridin' days was the best Irishman in the business. Meet Michael Costello, ex-jock!"

The man extended a large hand to Alec. "Belmont be a long way off and the bus late," he said wearily. " 'Tis a good turn I'm owin' ye both."

Henry drove the van out into the traffic again. "Don't be so formal, Mike. What're you doin' here anyway? The last time I saw you you were trainin' a stable on the Coast."

" 'Tis the truth ye speak, Henry. But I near bored meself to death with it."

"Bored?" Henry asked incredulously, taking his eyes for a second off the busy thoroughfare.

"So I took to ridin' again," the wiry man went on. "Sure, an' why not? What ails ye, Henry? Why do ye look at me with such grand surprise in your eyes? Why should I quit ridin' for good? I get just as much of a kick out of it as I iver did, ye know. And if I do say so meself 'tis not the touch I've lost with the reins. Yesterday I rode the great Casey in the best race of me life. 'Tis not forgettin' it I'll be!"

Henry pulled the van over to the side of the street and stopped. Then he turned slowly to Michael Costello. "C-Casey . . . you rode Casey in the Metropolitan?"

The wiry man shut his eyes, then opened them. "Henry, what ails ye? Why do ye stop while Belmont still be a long way off?"

"But you rode Casey . . ." Henry repeated.

"Sure, and a great horse he's makin' of himself," the man said while filling his pipe. His round, wrinkled face with its very black eyes turned to Alec. " 'Tis the truth I speak about Casey, for Henry will bear me out that once I rode Man o' War. There never was a horse like him until yesterday. I'm expectin' great things from Casey."

When Alec said nothing the man turned back to Henry and added, "From Casey *and me.* 'Tis likin' the ride I gave him they are and no one else will sit on him but me. Now 'tis later in the mornin' than I like to be gettin' to work even for a Sunday. So please get on with you."

Henry started the van but remained silent a long time

while Alec and Michael Costello talked to each other. Finally the trainer said without taking his gaze from the road, "Alec—"

"Yes, Henry?"

"Forget what I said about changin' the name of the farm, will you? It seems there's a lot of run left in some of the old boys. That had better include me if I'm goin' to look Mike in the eye from now on."

Joy swept over Alec and he grabbed Michael Costello's thick arm in gratitude.

" 'Tis too tight ye are holdin' me arm," the wiry man shouted.

Henry looked at his old friend and chuckled. Just ahead loomed the great grandstand of Belmont Park.

1 Pound = 1 Neck

10

The first light of morning seeped between the slats of the Venetian blinds as Alec reached for the ringing alarm clock beside his bed and snapped it off. He lay in bed for another minute, resenting these early-morning risings and yet fully aware that it wouldn't be the same wonderful life without them.

He turned and looked at Henry, who was in the other bed, asleep and snoring. Alec knew how much his friend appreciated clean-smelling sheets and a comfortable bed after many nights of sleeping in the van. Henry had good accommodations at Belmont and that was one reason the trainer was glad to be back.

They had a good deal at Belmont was more like it, Alec thought.

He heard someone stirring in the kitchen downstairs. Don or Mrs. Conover must be getting breakfast. He'd better be up and out, too. But he remained in bed, still half-asleep and

wondering why he'd had such an awful night. It wasn't like
him to toss nervously about for so many hours before finally
going to sleep.

Wednesday. This *was* Wednesday, wasn't it? They'd arrived Sunday and had settled in. Monday he'd walked the
filly and galloped the Black. Tuesday he'd breezed him a
slow four furlongs and the Black had fought his snug hold
every inch of the way. The filly wasn't going to be breezed
until the latter part of the week. Henry had decided to give
her a short rest after the Preakness, maybe in the hope that
she'd forget Wintertime if she didn't join him on the track.

Alec rolled over to the edge of the bed and sat up. He was
still a little groggy from the last hour's deep sleep. So this
had to be Wednesday, he decided.

Then it was race day for the Black!

The cold, bare facts woke him up as nothing else would
have done. The Speed Handicap at seven-eighths of a mile.
There would be ten starters, with the Black having been assigned top weight of 130 pounds. Henry hadn't liked giving
as much as 20 pounds to the nearest weighted horse but he'd
kept the Black in the race.

"Only seven furlongs," the trainer had said, "so he ought
to be able to handle it and still beat 'em."

A purse of $8,950 would go to the winner. That amount
plus what Black Minx had earned in the Preakness would
make a grand total of $20,200, Alec figured. Still a long way
from the necessary $100,000 for the new barn but they were
on their way.

He went to the window. "Stop counting purses before
we've won them," he grunted.

Now that Alec realized what day it was he knew the reason for his bad night. He never slept well the night before a race. It was due to all the excitement preceding an important contest. Every rider, every athlete, knew it well. There was nothing unique about it.

Alec never for a moment considered the grim possibilities of sudden injury and even death as the reason for his sleeplessness. Jockeys never thought along those lines if they wanted to stay in the saddle. They got down fast and became anything but jockeys, knowing full well that a nervous race rider was very close to being a dead or injured one.

Only the spectators standing on the rail near the first turn had any idea what it was really like. They were the ones who could see the crowding of horses and men as racers slammed hard against one another and riders grabbed anything to keep from going down under tons of steel-shod hoofs. But a jockey never thought about that.

Alec stood quietly in the grayness of his room and thought, *This is the big day, and I'm as ready to go as he is. All I've lost is a few hours' sleep. It's happened before. It'll happen again.*

Whoever was in the kitchen below had the radio on and was getting the weather report. "Fair and mild today with a high of sixty-five. . . ."

May 26. A perfect spring day. A dry, fast track for the Black.

Alec quietly raised the Venetian blinds and the light poured into the room. Henry stirred, grunted, and Alec said, "It's six."

Henry turned over and went back to sleep.

It doesn't matter this morning. So sleep, Henry, sleep. The Black isn't going anywhere until this afternoon. The filly can be galloped

*later in the morning. Just feed and talk and muck out stalls.
That's all we have to do.*

Looking out the window, Alec saw Wintertime being
turned out in the small paddock between the house and
barn. The blood bay colt had been a little off his feed, so
Don Conover had started giving him a few hours of freedom
in the small paddock every morning. He didn't want Wintertime to go track sour on him with the rich Belmont
Stakes coming up.

Alec wondered if the trouble might be that the colt
missed Black Minx, who was stabled on the other side of the
barn. Silly notion, of course. Maybe his thoughts about the
whole affair were ridiculous. Still, weren't horses supposed to
be treated like people? Wasn't that what Henry always said?

Alec watched Peek-a-Boo, the Shetland pony owned by
Don's six-year-old daughter, being led into the paddock to
join Wintertime.

From the kitchen window below came the smells of coffee
and bacon and toast. Alec was hungry but the appetizing
aroma of good food didn't bother him as it did some of the
riders he knew. And he knew too that once a jockey starts
fighting his appetite and the scales he'd better start looking
for another job.

His eyes left the small chestnut pony for the stablemen
who were already raking the ground around the barn. Everything here was neat and clean and freshly painted. Like the
tack trunks, the pails, brooms and rakes were painted red and
green, the colors of Jean Parshall's racing stable. So were the
big sliding doors to the barn as well as the paddock fencing.
This was *permanent* headquarters for Miss Parshall's stable.
Unlike Alec and Henry, she had no farm of her own and her
horses seldom left Belmont Park to race outside the New

York area. The exceptions, of course, were the Kentucky Derby and the Preakness.

"I'm a city girl," Alec had heard her tell Henry once, "and Belmont is far enough out in the country to keep my horses. I'll let you fellows run the farms."

In a way, Alec decided, she had just about everything here that one could have at a farm except for the broodmares and young stock. There were acres upon acres of lovely towering shade trees, and at all times of the year the wonderful smell of hay and horses. Many stables made Belmont their permanent home and had quarters such as these.

Alec went into the bathroom and washed. Yes, as Henry had said, "It was good to be back at Belmont." And it was good of Don Conover to take them and their horses into his home and barn. They would not have been so comfortable stabled in transient quarters.

After dressing in jeans and a light sweater, Alec left the room without awakening Henry. He went down the back stairs and outside. Usually Alec had coffee with Don and Mrs. Conover but this morning was different. He preferred being alone as much as possible today—alone with his horse.

Wintertime and the Shetland pony came to the fence when they saw him. Alec parted the pony's heavy forelock so he could see her bright eyes. "Peek-a-boo yourself," he said, smiling.

Going on to the barn, he slid open the red-and-green trimmed door and went inside.

" 'Morning, Ray," he called. The man he greeted had a rub rag swinging from his left back pocket and he was raking the walking turf under the shed.

" 'Morning, Alec. The boss comin' along?"

"Pretty soon now. He was having breakfast when I left

the house." Alec went down the corridor, and some of the horses stretched their heads over the stall doors so he could pat them.

The stableman called after him, "I 'spect you got no taste for breakfast this morning?"

"Never knew a morning that I couldn't eat, Ray," Alec answered without turning around. But he knew he wasn't fooling Ray or himself. He wasn't hungry at all.

An exercise boy turned from the training sheet posted outside the tack stall. "With the Black carrying a hundred and thirty pounds this afternoon, I guess you can eat all you want," he said. His remark was made jokingly but there was great respect in his voice as well. He looked upon Alec Ramsay as his ideal. Someday he hoped to be as good a rider.

Alec stopped at the tack room. "Sam," he said, smiling, "you and I could ride him together and still make that weight."

"Plus two seven-course meals," Ray called from down the corridor.

The exercise boy said, "That would be the day, the day I put a leg up on the Black!"

Alec went to the other side of the barn and there he found the filly with her head above the half-door. He refilled her water pail and then went into the next stall. "Hello," he said quietly. "This is your day."

The tall stallion came quickly to him and Alec's eyes swept approvingly over his great body. The Black had lost what little extra weight he'd had upon his return to the track. Now he was in fine trim, the embodiment of a sleek and powerful machine. He would give a good account of himself today. There was some straw in his thick mane and tail, evidence that he'd been down on the floor during the night. That was good. It rested him to have the weight taken off his feet. He'd need all the energy he had today. His eyes were clear and quiet, reflecting the calmness of his whole being. Not until he was on his way to the paddock would the first marks of perspiration appear on his body.

As Alec picked the straw from the Black's mane he couldn't help thinking how everything about his horse spelled greatness—*true* greatness and not something labeled "great" one season and forgotten the next. That was why Sam had spoken with awe at just the thought of riding him. And that was why everybody called the Black by his right name and not some nickname. It was unusual around a stable for a horse to be called by the name that appeared on his registration papers and in racing programs. For example, Eclipse was "Pops"; Wintertime was "Red"; Black Minx was "Baby"; Golden Vanity was "Sunny"; and Silver Jet was "Bud."

"Only Casey is 'Casey'," Alec said aloud. "I wonder if that means anything. But that's enough. I'd better get to work."

A short time later Alec left the barn, going out by another door to avoid meeting anybody. Beyond the high hedge that guarded the track he could hear the muffled thunder of a horse coming down the stretch. Closing his ears to it he walked still faster, scarcely seeing the men and horses who passed him on their way to the big track. He nodded only when friends called to him.

On another morning it would have been different. But this was race day. Even more important, it was *the Black's day.* Alec felt the nervous perspiration trickle down the sides of his chest and he chided himself. "At least the Black waits until he's on the way to the paddock before sweating. Take it easy. The race is still hours away."

He went on and began whistling in the cool morning air. He wasn't fooling anyone.

"That's Alec Ramsay," he heard one stableboy say to another while they were walking hot horses clothed in bright coolers. "He and the Black are going today. The third race, I think it is."

He passed between the long rows of barns and thought how big and neat and somehow formidable Belmont was. High wrought-iron fences and well-guarded gates separated it from the rest of the world.

Perhaps, he decided, it was all this elegance and bigness that caused Belmont Park to put itself above such matters as exploiting the Black's appearance in the day's feature handicap. Other than a single publicity release to the press announcing the names of the ten horses going to the post in the Speed Handicap, nothing had been done. Belmont Park's treatment of the Black's return to the races was certainly devoid of any sensationalism.

"That's the way it should be," Alec recalled telling Henry.

"Maybe so," Henry had answered. "But I would have liked to hear the clash of cymbals, and you can bet we'd have heard 'em at any other track where he might have raced, especially on the West Coast. It would have been a production there, a real Hollywood-type job! Still," he added resignedly, "I guess this is what makes Belmont what it is. Maybe that's why it's home."

Alec pushed through the crowd in the busy track kitchen. He ordered bacon and eggs, aware that many eyes were on him and wishing now that he hadn't come at all.

"I'm like a kid riding his first race," he thought. "And for the life of me I can't stop myself. Just thinking about going to the post with the Black again has me all on edge, worse than ever before."

A few minutes later he left the kitchen without finishing his breakfast.

That afternoon he arrived late in the jockeys' room. Those who were riding the first race had already dressed and gone. He went to his locker and sat down on the bench.

"Well, 'tis a worried face you're wearin', Alec," a familiar voice said.

"Hello, Mike," Alec answered, looking up. The man's twinkling black eyes made him smile too. "I'm not really worried. That's just my usual face."

"Begone with ye." Michael Costello chuckled. " 'Tis the other I know better."

The jockeys who had been listening laughed and one of them, mimicking an Irish brogue, shouted with mock excitement in his voice, "Alec's a nervous *mon* today, Mike. He's a-ridin' the Black!"

"Hold your tongue!" The wiry old man's command had an immediate effect, for the others became quiet and returned to their lockers. Then he winked at Alec and said, " 'Tis ridin' ye like an apprentice they are today."

"That's what I feel like, Mike," Alec confessed.

"Faith, you'll not be around us long on the likes of him!"

Alec smiled. "I didn't know you were riding the third race," he said.

" 'Tis the truth ye speak. A plodder named Earl of Sykes, who has no more right to be in the race than he has to such a title. Now if 'twere Casey I was a-ridin' you'd never get free from us."

"When's Casey going?" Alec asked.

"Monday's Suburban."

The man began undressing at his locker and Alec noticed that, unlike Henry, Michael Costello had no trouble keeping his weight down. He was as thin as an iron rail and just as hard.

"What weight are you making today, Mike?" Alec asked.

"One hundred and ten," the man answered. " 'Tis twenty pounds ye're givin' us. That by me personal rule-of-thumb method makes you ridin' the better horse by five lengths."

Alec smiled. "A pound a neck, you mean?"

The man turned his round, wrinkled face to Alec. " 'Tis a long neck, me boy, as I figger it. A quarter of a length for each pound or four pounds for the length of his whole body. Ye won't find a better yardstick than that up to a mile and an eighth."

"Then the twenty extra pounds we're carrying should bring us down to the wire together," Alec said lightly, "so don't be sad."

" 'Tis what the track handicapper thinks, not I," Michael Costello corrected, turning back to his locker. " 'Tis the truth I speak when I say the Black is more than five lengths better than the best of us. But who am I to put meself above the good, hard-workin' mon in the office who's doin' his best to equalize the field?"

Some of the jockeys left the room for the second race and Alec said no more. He wouldn't have much longer to wait. By now Henry and Napoleon must be taking the Black to the paddock.

Alec finished dressing and once more turned to Michael Costello. He watched the man pull on his skin-tight white nylon pants. Still hanging in the locker were the rich blue-and-gold silks of the famous Milkyway Stable, owner of

Casey as well as Earl of Sykes. Alec knew that such a large and popular stable wouldn't be represented in the Speed Handicap unless it felt it had a good chance of winning, regardless of Mike's criticism of his *plodding* mount.

For a moment Alec watched the little man who had made the waiting period in the jockey room a lot easier than it might have been. He was anxious, too, to ride against Michael Costello after all he'd been told about him.

"There never was a headier rider than Mike," Henry had said, "but few people except trainers were ever actually aware of it. Mike never did anything during a race that labeled him as a spectacular rider. Instead, he made his moves so quietly and without fanfare that he'd suddenly appear in front and people in the stands would wonder how they'd missed seein' him get up there! So would the other jocks.

"And another thing," Henry went on. "Mike never did anything mean. He was clean and fair to those ridin' against him, and he followed orders better than any rider I've ever known. He never tried to prove that he was smarter than the trainer who'd given him a fit horse to ride. All in all Mike was a well-liked guy by everybody—owners, trainers and jockeys. I'm sure he still is. But if he ever races against you, be on your toes or you'll find yourself out on a limb and wonderin' how you ever got there! Just remember he's got a bag of tricks that's taken a lifetime to learn. He's in good physical shape, too, so in many ways he's more dangerous now than ever before. I wish I could be ridin' against him. It's no easy job."

Alec turned back to his locker. "I'll be on my toes," he said aloud, without thinking.

"What's that ye say?" the wiry man asked.

"Nothing," Alec answered, standing up to retuck his

black silks into the top of his pants. Then he took his goggles and fitted them over his white cap before putting it on his head. "Just talking to myself," he explained.

Michael Costello shrugged his narrow shoulders. But his twinkling black eyes belied his apparent disinterest in either Alec Ramsay or the race to come.

Alec closed his locker and followed most of the other jockeys in the third race out of the room. He knew Michael Costello wouldn't be far behind him.

One pound was one neck.

Speed!

11

Thirty minutes before post time Alec walked into the scale room to join the line of jockeys who were weighing out for the third race. There were eight riders ahead of him, which meant that only Michael Costello was missing. Soon he, too, came into the room and stood behind Alec.

The line of riders moved faster toward the official scale. A valet named Victor Hasluck was waiting for Alec. He and the other jockey valets were supplied by the track, for a fee of two dollars each, to assist the riders with their tack. Victor held Henry's battle-scarred saddle in his arms.

Alec stepped forward, taking his tack from Victor. Beneath the old saddle was the special pad whose empty pockets would now be filled with heavy strips of lead.

"Ramsay," the valet told the Clerk of the Scales. "Number three."

Alec stepped onto the scale. From his original weight of 110 pounds the arrow ascended as the lead was added to the saddle pad. Finally the arrow came to a stop.

"Thirty," the clerk said. "Ramsay. Number three. One hundred and thirty. Check."

Alec stepped off the scale, handing his tack back to Victor. As he went to the number rack to pick up his 3 he heard the only other valet left in the room say, "Costello. Number four."

Alec put his number high on his arm and then looked around at the scale. He noted the martingale that Mike was holding. It too must be weighed as a part of Earl of Sykes's "clothing."

Alec went on to the door while the clerk said, "Ten. Costello. Number four. One hundred and ten."

Twenty pounds of "dead" weight is the difference between us, Alec thought. *But it will take more than that to beat the Black!*

Michael Costello caught up to Alec just outside the room.

"Is it ridin' in Henry's old saddle ye are?" he asked, his black eyes looking hard at the boy.

Alec nodded but didn't stop, for he was anxious to reach the paddock. In his haste he left the man behind.

"I am a-promisin'," Mike called after him, "that with such a saddle yer good fortune will come with mine."

A strange friend, Alec decided. But he must remember what Henry had said. *"Watch him. Be on your toes every second."*

Alec stepped out of the building and then stopped. Coming up the tree-lined lane which led from the stable area to the paddock was the Black accompanied by Henry astride Napoleon. Henry was wearing his new broad-brimmed hat but he might as well have had on his battered old one for all the attention he was getting. Everybody along the lane was looking at the Black. As the stallion approached the saddling shed a roar of applause came from the heavily banked crowd on the other side of the paddock's iron fence.

Mike stood behind Alec and said, " 'Tis a lot of horse ye have there but he's scarin' nobody or ye wouldn't be up against such a large field."

It was quiet within the confines of the paddock compared to the noise on the other side of the fence. Alec passed the open stalls until he had reached the Black. There were people gathered around the stall whom he didn't know, but he recognized them as track officials and owners and friends of friends. They were standing as close to the stall as possible, their voices low, almost in whispers, while they talked to one another and to Henry. They had eyes only for the tall black stallion.

Alec took the tack from Victor, who was standing nearby, and went into the stall. "Hello, Black," Alec said softly, his hands finding his horse. Now everything was going to be all right, very much all right. His nervousness never lasted long once the tack went on.

Henry took the leaded saddle pad from Alec. "It's not light but it won't stop him today. Nothing will, not in this field."

Alec nodded toward the adjacent stall. "How about Mike's horse?"

"No. But watch Mike for tricks. He's clean but tough. He won't give you an inch." Turning to the people outside the stall, Henry asked them to move farther back. Then he turned back to Alec, grunting, "It's a small army we have here."

Alec watched only the Black. The stallion's coat had already broken out with little spots of perspiration and there was lather between his hind legs. Also, he'd started digging in the dirt with his right foreleg. Alec talked to him quietly while Henry put on the white saddle cloth with the large black 3.

"Don't let Mike high-ball it out of the gate and then gradually sneak back, makin' you think he's settin' a blistering race when he isn't," the trainer warned. "That's an old trick of his, an' he'll use anything to stay in front. Remember this is only seven furlongs. Don't take hold of the Black enough to make him shake his head. Get out in front and keep goin'. He's ready for this race, more ready than the handicapper thinks he is or he'd be carryin' a lot more weight. That's just between you and me," he added hastily.

Alec nodded in complete agreement. The Black was ready to go. No doubt about it. The flesh was drawn smooth and tight over his whole body and the muscles stood out hard and clean and strong. His long legs were unblemished. Most important of all was the look in his eyes. Excitement was there, of course, but eagerness as well—an eagerness to get on with this business; he was tired of waiting.

Alec stroked the Black while Henry finished saddling. A bell sounded and the first horse left his stall for the walking ring a short distance from the saddling shed. Behind him came his entourage—his jockey, trainer and owner.

Alec turned to Michael Costello's mount, who was leaving his stall. A dark bay and not a very pretty horse. But racing machines didn't need to be pretty to be fast and this was such a horse. Alec couldn't find fault with his conformation and he had to admit he'd never seen more perfect shoulders.

"Are you sure about him?" he asked Henry, nodding toward Earl of Sykes. "He looks awfully good to me."

"He won't bother you," Henry answered brusquely. "If you're goin' to worry, worry about the Black. Make sure you keep him in line. A lot of people don't think you can. Come on."

Alec led the stallion from his stall. He wasn't worrying about controlling the Black or anything else. The waiting had ended and so had his nervousness. "Let's get to it," he told Henry impatiently.

There were people on either side of the path that led to the walking ring and Alec heard them repeat over and over again, "That's the Black. That's him. Right there. You can reach out and touch him!"

To keep everything under control, Henry had once more mounted Napoleon and was using the old gelding's big body to keep away people as well as other horses. No one got very close with Napoleon's well-trained hindquarters moving as they did.

Alec stepped lightly on the tanbark of the walking ring. It was more crowded there, for every runner had his little group of well-wishers. They stood in the shade of old maple trees while jockeys received last-minute instructions. Outside the confines of the ring the spectators pushed hard against one another and called to horses and trainers and jockeys alike. But it was the Black they watched most of all and they wondered if he would provide a race worthy of the loud ovation they'd given him. Within a few minutes they would know. Already the Black was looking over their heads in the direction of the great stands.

"Riders up!" the paddock judge called.

Henry boosted Alec onto the Black and then remounted Napoleon. "Let's go get the money, son," he said quietly.

As they were leaving the walking ring Alec turned to the huge statue of Man o' War that was there. Someday, perhaps, the Black too would be immortalized in such a way. But not now. There was still too much racing to be done!

The crowd was lined up along the ropes all the way to the edge of the track. When the horses stepped onto the cocoa-colored oval a wave of applause swept the reserved section nearest them and then it flowed the length of the clubhouse and grandstand until it became one sustained roar.

"Do you think that's for him?" Alec asked Henry. The Black shifted, almost slipping out from under him.

The trainer grunted while moving Napoleon closer to the Black. "Who else?" he finally said. "They don't need a public-address announcement to recognize *him*. But he'd better be good after all this build-up."

"He'll be good," Alec promised confidently.

"If he is, maybe you'd better not win by too much. Once you know you've got the race sewed up take back on him some. If we win by too many lengths he'll be carryin' that much more lead the next time out. Let's keep the handicapper guessin'. We're doin' better than I expected."

"Okay, Henry."

"But watch Mike every second," the trainer warned. "If his horse has just one punch in him he'll use it at the right time. Ridin' is an art with him, not just talent."

"Okay, Henry."

"What else can I tell you? Y'know more about it than I do. He's your horse."

"Okay, Henry."

Alec was listening only to the soft plops of the Black's

hoofs in the deep, plushy going. Not that the track was slow by any means. It hadn't rained all week and the top soil was thoroughly dry. The deep cushion was soft and easy on a horse's feet. Some liked it, some didn't. The Black was one of those who did, Alec knew. He'd run as well here as he would over a hard, fast strip.

The marshal led the parade going up the homestretch. Belmont Park provided no music, no color, no fuss. Here were simply ten entries going to the post for the running of the day's feature handicap. The only noticeable difference between this race and others on the program was that the applause continued, moving along with the parade and erupting loudly when the Black passed.

Belmont Park made it easier for the spectators to *see* the horses going to the post than was possible at most other tracks. Henry wasn't the only stable rider who was leading from the right side today. There were seven other ponies accompanying the racers and all were on the off side so they wouldn't hide the runners. This was done at the insistence of the track management.

Alec watched the horse in front of him go into a slow gallop past the stands, showing the crowd his movements in action. This, too, the management insisted upon. Alec waited until the horse had slowed to a walk again and then nodded to Henry. "Okay," he said. "Let's go."

The trainer clucked to Napoleon. "Come on, old bones," he said. "Show 'em you can still beat it out."

Napoleon went forward and the Black slid easily along beside him. Alec kept a tight hold but the stallion didn't pull or shake his head and his great eyes were on the crowd. He was curious but not alarmed. Alec brought him to a stop with Napoleon.

They walked a short distance and then behind them Alec heard the heavy thud of hoofs. Another horse was being galloped. The hoofs rang hard and were coming a little too close, he thought. He was about to turn to see who it was when Napoleon suddenly lashed out with his hind legs, throwing Henry forward in his saddle.

The Black bolted at the sudden activity on his right. Alec went with him and the lead shank between the Black and Henry was almost pulled from the man's hands. But Henry held on to it, swinging the Black around Napoleon. Then Alec saw what had happened.

The Milkyway stable pony had galloped too close to them and Napoleon had kicked out, sending him against Earl of Sykes, who had gone down and was now sprawled on the track! Even as Alec saw the entangled horse and rider he was off the Black and rushing to Michael Costello's aid.

The jockey's left leg hung in a stirrup and every time his horse moved, attempting to get up, the leg was twisted.

Alec straddled the horse, keeping his head turned sideways and down on the track so he wouldn't try to get up again. He soothed the frightened animal as best he could, then spoke to Mike. "Can you pull your leg out now?" he asked.

"I can if ye get a bit more of his weight on your side or if my pony boy just shows the same kind of speed. . . ." Looking for his stable rider and finding him watching, he shouted, "Come on with you! 'Tis a far cry from bein' a competent pony boy ye are! Help young Alec!"

By that time the track's outriders were there and Alec had all the assistance he needed to get Mike free. The old jockey got to his feet, brushing the others' hands away. "Let me be," he said self-consciously. "I'm all right, I tell ye." His horse was up and unhurt.

"Thank ye, Alec," Mike said. " 'Tis another good turn I'm owin' ye." To the outrider he added, "Now leg me up if ye will and we'll get on with the race. 'Tis enough time we've wasted."

A few minutes later the field approached the starting gate on the far side of the track.

Henry said, "Go to it, Alec. I'll be waiting at the other end."

It wasn't necessary for the starter's ground crew to assist Alec in getting the Black into the gate. The stallion went eagerly into the number 3 stall, jumping the shadow cast by the closed wire-mesh flaps in front.

The others went quickly inside too. After the accident and the resultant delay in getting to the post, the starter wanted to get the horses off fast. Alec straightened the Black's head. "Now, boy," he said. "We won't be long. Steady now."

There was plenty of racing room, for the track was wide and big. A mile and a half of it all around. The seven-furlong race would start directly across the track from the finish line. They were a half-mile away from the spectators, with high trees, hedges, steeplechase barriers and even a lake between them. The fans low in the stands might have complaints about not being able to see the complete race, but Alec had none. It was the best track in the country for the Black.

"Horses for courses," was the old rhyme, and this even, deep-cushioned track suited the stallion's strides to perfection.

In the stall on Alec's right, Michael Costello was flung against the padded sides by his uneasy mount. He got him straightened out and shouted, " 'Tis a poor excuse for a horse ye are. Ye can't stay on your own four feet!"

Alec laughed at Mike's angry outburst and the old jockey,

hearing him, said without taking his eyes off the track, " 'Tis the truth I speak, Alec. I have ye to thank for . . ."

He never finished, for the bell clanged and the stall doors flew open.

The Black came out of the gate as eagerly as he'd gone into it. He was bubbling over with desire to run and seemingly unaware of the presence of other horses.

Alec let the reins slide through his hands. It had been at the farm where he'd last allowed the great stallion to go all out with him. Alec's hands suddenly tightened on the reins again. He squeezed rather than pulled as a horse swerved dangerously in front of them and stayed there.

From across the infield came the distant roar of the crowd, but Alec listened only to the steady plop-plop of the Black's hoofs passing lightly over the soft, dry dirt. He looked only in front of him, waiting for the track to clear. Three furlongs to the long, sweeping quarter-of-a-mile curve! His grip on the reins tightened still more and then he began pulling back to avoid the horse directly in his path. The Black didn't like the snug hold at all.

"Don't take hold enough to make him shake his head," Henry had ordered. *"Get out in front and keep going."*

Alec swung the Black around the horse ahead and set him free! Before them was the empty track he'd wanted. Now there would be nothing to this race but a great black stallion! Alec sat down to ride and the resounding drum of other horses' hoofs slipped rapidly behind him.

If the Black kept going all out, how many additional pounds would he be assigned in the richer, more important handicaps to come? Alec asked himself. *Wouldn't it be far wiser to win by just a length or two? Hadn't Henry so instructed me during those last few minutes before the race?*

Under Alec now was twenty pounds of lead. Enough of it could stop a freight train, much less the Black. Alec had seen a few extra pounds mean the difference between winning and losing a rich race, especially over the longer distances when the "dead" weight became heavier and heavier with each stride. Alec took up on the reins and the Black, shaking his head vigorously, shortened his strides.

Alec gently eased him over to the rail. The long banked curve was just beyond and soon they'd be in front of the grandstand. Alec couldn't have asked for anything better. The race was going as he wanted it to go. They were winning but not by so many lengths as to impress anybody, especially the handicapper.

They swept into the turn, tipping to the left of the banked track that rose high and wide on the outside. It was strangely quiet. Alec could hear the steady beat of hoofs, the Black's and those of the other horses behind him, but not the roar from the stands. He saw the spectators on their feet. He knew they were yelling as they always did when a field of horses approached the stretch run. Yet he could not hear them—only the hoofs.

Suddenly there came an urgent, faster beat and then far on his right, high on the banked turn, sped a dark bay horse. Riding him for all he was worth, using hands, legs and whip, was Michael Costello!

Before Alec could touch the Black, Mike came winging down the graded dirt road and slipped in front of them! Within the whip of an eyelash the lead had changed hands!

"Watch Mike every second," Henry had said. *"If that 'plodder' of his has just one punch in him he'll use it at the right time. Ridin' is an art with him, not just talent."*

The veteran jockey was hustling Earl of Sykes along, all

right, just as Henry had warned. Alec wasn't worried. In one easy jump he could take the Black past Mike's mount again. He waited until they were nearing the end of the turn and the track was beginning to straighten out, then he reached for the Black's right shoulder.

Now Alec could hear the roar of the crowd. He also heard the race announcer call out through the public-address system, "That's Earl of Sykes in front. The Black is second and starting his move. Iron Man and Hell's Fury are coming up fast on the outside. . . ."

Alec heard nothing more, for suddenly Mike Costello was no longer rocking in his saddle or urging his horse on. Instead he slowed Earl of Sykes and Alec had to shove his feet hard against the stirrup irons, almost standing in them to keep the Black from running over the bay leader. At that second, too, he realized he couldn't pull out and go around, for now on his right were Iron Man and Hell's Fury, who had come up. The track had straightened out. Alec knew what a world of speed he had under him *but there was no place to go*!

He decided he must take up on the Black and go around all three horses while he still had time. Suddenly Mike began moving in his saddle again and Earl of Sykes surged in front of the other two horses. The Black snorted in rage and frustration and went after him. Alec felt him grab the bit. Now there was no chance of pulling him up and going around the two horses on his right. In one magnificent leap the Black set out after the hard-running bay leader directly in his path!

But Michael Costello, Alec found, was not finished with his bag of tricks. No sooner did the veteran jockey have Earl of Sykes a length in front of the two horses on his right than he quit hustling and steered a course that left no room for the Black to get through between them.

"Be on your toes every second," Henry had warned Alec. Instead Mike had caught him *flat-footed*!

They had reached the beginning of the long stands. Alec figured he still might have time to take up and go all the way around. It would be awfully close but they could do it.

"Come on, Black!"

But instead of doing as Alec's hands and voice had directed, the tall stallion, his teeth hard on the bit, made a direct line for the small gap between the bay leader's haunches and the two racing horses on his right.

Alec knew there was not enough room to go through. Yet the stallion's strides increased in tempo and scope. He seemed unmindful of the bay's flaying hind legs. *There was no hole but the Black was going to try to make one!*

Alec shouted repeatedly, "Go on, Mike! Give us room!"

The old jockey glanced back. He saw the Black's head just off his mount's hindquarters and sudden surprise showed in his eyes. He glanced at the two other horses. But he made no attempt to move his mount faster. He was going to stay where he was, certain that the pocket would hold and that the race would be his.

Suddenly the earth erupted about Michael Costello and his horse! Instead of an empty track on his right, he saw a giant black horse. Mike went for his whip, knowing that the pocket was no longer there and that somehow the Black had broken through, making a hole where there had been none at all.

The veteran rider shouted to his horse, not expecting by any means to catch the Black, who was already many lengths beyond and drawing ever farther away. Now all Mike wanted was to finish ahead of the others. He had tried hard to win this race but, after all, a jock couldn't ride a winner every time out. Monday would be different. Monday was Memorial Day. Monday would be Casey's Day.

The Big Apple

12

The Belmont Park management called its feature race on Memorial Day "America's Greatest Handicap." That year everyone else called it *"Casey's* Suburban."

The day itself set a record for high temperature and humidity. Casey took care of the rest of the records. He beat the largest field ever to go to the post for the Suburban since 1884. He broke the track and race record for the distance of a mile and a quarter, a mark set in 1913, which no one had ever taken seriously because it had been made before electric timers were used. He carried 132 pounds on his back, giving up to 25 pounds to the lightest-weighted horses in the field. He earned a record purse of more than $70,000.

If the crowd of 65,343 persons at the track had been polled, it is doubtful that any among them could have named the horses who finished second and third in the race, some fifteen lengths behind Casey. All eyes were on the winner even long after he had swept under the wire—and for racetrack fans that was some kind of a record in itself.

Alec and Henry stood on the graveled apron before the stands and waited for Casey to return to the winner's circle. The place was packed solid. They couldn't have left the area if they'd wanted to.

Henry grunted. "I don't mind not bein' able to wiggle but I would like to breathe."

Alec kept his eyes on the tall, easy-moving chestnut horse coming across the track. Casey wasn't having any trouble breathing. He looked as if he could do it all over again. A red-coated outrider was alongside Casey, holding the bridle. Mike Costello was grinning as though the winner's purse of $73,000 were all his. A part of it was—ten percent. Mike's eyes were as bright as the lighted board in the center field. He had seen the record time posted there, the big numerals 1:59 4/5. That was why he was grinning. Who wouldn't be, in his place? No horse was supposed to have been capable of going that fast on this strip of sandy loam. But Casey had done it. Casey and Costello. He was a very strange little old man, Alec decided.

" 'Tis a good turn I'm owin' ye," Mike had promised twice, Alec recalled. Once when he and Henry had picked him up at the bus stop. Again, when he, Alec, had picked him up off the track. But Mike hadn't given an inch in return when he'd asked for it. According to Henry it was good race riding to keep a hole closed. But he would have opened up for Mike or for any other rider when he'd seen there was no stopping a horse from "bulling" his way through as the Black had done last Wednesday.

Casey's groom walked onto the track to take over from the outrider. He led the chestnut horse and its rider into the winner's enclosure. Mike sat still, his black eyes twinkling while he patted Casey and cameras clicked away.

"We could have made a real race of it," Henry said. "Not just a breeze-in for him like it was."

"We could have beaten him," Alec said.

"Maybe."

"No maybes," Alec insisted.

"Later in the season maybe," Henry said. "He's pretty sharp right now."

"I wish we could have been in it," Alec said quietly. "We'd have shown him. Seventy-three thousand dollars' worth of showing it would've been. Just this one race and we'd have had a new barn."

Henry chuckled at the boy's persistence. "We'd have been in it all right if you'd told me on March fifteenth, when nominations for this race closed, that our barn was goin' to burn down early in May. We'd not only have been in it but we'd have had the Black *ready* for it."

"He's ready anyway," Alec said confidently. His eyes remained on Casey. A top horse, he reminded himself, make no mistake about that. Maybe even a great one after today. He traveled. He really did. Mike had said that Casey was a great horse. Mike knew great horses from on top. Mike had ridden Man o' War.

But Mike had never ridden the Black. So Mike didn't know everything.

"By the same token," Alec said aloud, "I've never ridden Casey, so I don't know everything, either."

"What's that?" Henry asked, freeing a foot on which a man next to him had been stepping.

"I was wondering if we'd race Casey at Aqueduct," Alec said. The meeting at the nearby track would open in a couple of weeks and they had had time before the May 15 clos-

ing date to nominate the Black for some of its richest handicap races.

"I don't know," Henry answered. "Could be."

Alec watched Mike Costello get permission from the pre-
siding judge to dismount. No one was allowed near him as
he slipped off Casey's back and unsaddled his horse. Carrying
his tack, which included the heavy lead pad, he stepped onto
the scales in the enclosure, weighing in.

The Clerk of the Scales nodded as the arrow swung to the
same weight at which Costello had entered the race. "One
hundred thirty-two, check," the clerk said. The race was now
officially over.

Costello handed the tack to his valet and went back to
Casey, taking him from the groom. He wouldn't leave his
horse long enough to be interviewed by the television and
radio reporters and they wouldn't approach Casey. The
horse's nostrils were flared, not from heavy breathing, but
from excitement caused by the noisiness of the small enclosure. He let a hind leg go and the people behind him scat-
tered. His trainer and owner laughed but Mike remained
silently grim. The veteran jockey wanted to get his horse
back to the barn, Alec knew. Mike would let scarcely anyone
else touch Casey. He preferred to feed and take care of the
horse himself. No one else rode Casey, even in the mornings.

Who knows, thought Alec, *maybe that's why Casey's
shown such speed. It's happened before that a horse takes to
one particular person and does more for him than for anyone
else.*

Wasn't it so with the Black and himself?

Casey was put together much the same as the Black. He
was tall and light but very strong boned. He had an arched
bow in his neck and his head was all thoroughbred. His

shoulders were well sloped and he had a powerful set of hind muscles which ran down to low-set hocks. He was all power and beauty standing there in the circle—and judging from today's record race he was all speed as well.

"Let's get out of here," Henry said, "if we can." He began pushing and Alec followed him. They had received permission to work Black Minx between the seventh and eighth races on the day's program.

"When do you think we'll go against him?" Alec asked.

"Casey, you mean?"

Alec nodded and Henry said, "I dunno. A lot depends on the package they load on the Black. I'm not goin' to have them break 'im down with lead, not after Wednesday's exhibition. Why . . ."

Henry didn't finish. He didn't need to, for Alec knew well what he meant.

When a horse comes back as the Black had done and wins his first race by thirteen lengths in track record time, he is bound to be assigned a great deal more weight the next time out. It had been no secret that the Black had the bit hard against his teeth when he broke out of that pocket. Everyone had seen it, including the track handicapper.

Alec and Henry managed to get away from the packed stands and passed the paddock. They went down the lane toward the barns. Alec didn't take his eyes from the dirt path before them when he said, "I couldn't hold him back like you wanted me to. It was as if he'd stored up all this energy and then let it go all at once. He moved right up on Costello and said, 'One side, please!' *Bang!* We went through."

"Don't worry about it," Henry answered. "We'll make out all right. Besides, you rode 'im good. I never saw better coordination between horse and rider. You were with him."

Alec smiled. "Where else could I have gone?"

They stood to one side, watching the horses going to the paddock for the fifth race on the program.

Henry said, "Anyway, it was somethin' to see. I wasn't surprised so much by the Black's time as I was by the easy way he did it. Maybe he's sharper than I think he is."

"He's sharp, all right," Alec said as they continued down the path. "Is there any truth to the talk I've been hearing about a match race between Casey and the Black at equal weights?"

Henry nodded. "It's been more than just talk. We had an offer from a Jersey track for a $100,000 special match, winner-take-all basis at a mile and a quarter. I accepted but Casey's stable turned it down."

"Why?"

"I can only guess," Henry answered. "They probably figured there were enough big races ahead to keep them busy without goin' out and looking for trouble. Besides, it's easy enough for Casey and the Black to get together in a regular race. In fact they could meet in the Carter Handicap on July fourth."

Alec said, "But Casey would get the benefit of the weights."

"He might," Henry agreed. "I can't read the handicapper's mind. But there's one sure thing. I'm not goin' to take a chance of breakin' down the Black with lead. He's much too valuable."

Alec nodded in complete agreement and they passed through the stable area gate. Eclipse was in the nearest barn and they stopped to look at him.

"How's the big horse?" Henry asked the colt's trainer who was sitting at the open barn door.

"Oh, I think he'll live until we get him in the Belmont, Henry. Hello, Alec. Good race you rode Wednesday. Never did get a chance to tell you. Meant to, though. I really did."

"Thanks, Mr. Dawson," Alec said. Then with Henry he stepped just inside the barn. Both halves of Eclipse's stall door were open. "Aren't you afraid he'll get away from you?" Alec asked.

"No, we got well-trained horses 'round here," Dawson said quietly and unsmiling. "Not like most stables."

"You includin' us?" Henry belligerently asked his old friend. "You inferrin'—"

"I'm inferrin' nothin'," Dawson interrupted. "You're the one who's doin' the inferrin'."

Henry snorted contemptuously. "If we had two big fans blowin' up the air in each stall, maybe we could open our doors too and still keep the horses inside."

"Sure, they're smart. Horses know when they got it good, all right. But maybe you can't afford fans, Henry? Maybe you'd better hold on to that Derby money you won. It 'pears you won't be winnin' much more with that little old filly o' yours."

"Don't be too sure about that!" Henry answered. "Come on, Alec," he added abruptly. "Let's get out of here before we get so darn comfortable we can't do a decent job."

Alec hesitated, for he was studying Eclipse. He never got tired of looking at a horse and he always seemed to find something new. This fellow had a bow in his neck like the Black's, except that it was much thicker and shorter.

Eclipse's brown coat was so dark it was almost black. Yet in contrast he had lots of white on him, with a blaze running from forehead to nostrils, and long white stockings on

all four legs. His body was larger and more muscular than
either Casey's or the Black's. In fact, when he was standing
in his stall with his head down and his eyes half-closed, he
looked downright lazy and ponderous. But Alec knew that
that impression of him changed fast when Eclipse started
moving. In action the husky, towering colt was a picture of
perfect physical coordination.

Alec left the barn, thinking how rare it was to have such
top horses racing this year. The public, trainers and press
alike waited year after year for a *great* or even a *near-great*
horse to come along. Now they had Eclipse, a three-year-old
colt whom they proclaimed as "destined for greatness."
There was also Black Minx, who had proved how false was
the horsemen's proverb that "fillies don't win the Kentucky
Derby." Then there was Casey. After today's Suburban victory he was certain to be labeled "one of the greatest handicap stars of all time!" And, finally, the Black, a proven sire
and a great racehorse coming back from retirement. It
would be a year to be remembered by all who followed
racing.

Alec caught up with Henry. "Well," he said, "Eclipse
looks the way the Belmont winner is supposed to look."

"Yeah," Henry agreed. "Distance isn't going to stop that
horse. He won't have any trouble with a mile an' a half."

"Then you were kidding Mr. Dawson?" Alec asked. "You
don't think we have a chance of beating Eclipse with our
filly?"

"Let's see how she works today, Alec, then ask me again,"
Henry answered.

Between the seventh and eighth races Alec rode Black
Minx onto the track. There was a spontaneous roar of applause when the crowd saw her, for the newspapers had car-

ried the announcement of her public workout. She carried
her head higher than usual passing the stands, and her grace-
ful strides matched her regal bearing.

Henry had instructed Alec to go a half-mile in a slow
fifty-two seconds. He'd said he didn't want to ask much
speed of Black Minx just yet. The Belmont with its golden
purse was still two weeks off. Alec wondered if Henry was
delaying his request for speed because he was afraid she
wouldn't respond.

Alec and Henry had made a point of not letting Black
Minx see Wintertime either on the track or off. Neither he
nor Henry had ever discussed their own particular reasons
for handling the situation in such a way. They kept quiet
about it, knowing neither would understand the other
anyway.

Alec had watched Wintertime go more off his feed and
wondered if his own convictions were so ridiculous as they
seemed. Don Conover was becoming seriously worried
about his colt's lack of appetite and had stopped working
him altogether. Alec might have told the trainer what he
thought the trouble was but he didn't.

"Come, Baby," he said, sitting down in his saddle. "We
can move faster now."

They were on the backstretch with the huge stands a half-
mile away. Somewhere in that great holiday crowd was
Henry, unmindful of the day's heat and discomfort and with
his eyes narrowed, watching them.

"She's well seasoned with gallops," Henry had said in giving his instructions, "so don't snug her up too slow. Break
her off sharp and let her go against the bit. On the other
hand don't let her go faster than fifty-two. I don't want to
ask too much of her today. I just want to see how she goes.

Don't pull her up too sharp when you're done. Ease her off easy, nice and easy."

"Come, Baby," Alec repeated, clucking. To himself he said, *Sure, Henry, it's a cinch doing exactly what you ask. I can turn her off and on just like I was driving a car. Sure, Henry, sure. You know better. So do I. We talk just to hear ourselves talk sometimes.*

She was almost falling asleep on him. Couldn't she hear the noises of the crowd across the infield? They were yelling for her—or at least she ought to think so.

Slipping a heel across her girth, Alec said, "Come on, get on with you! If we're not careful we'll hold up the next race. The judges won't like that."

But Black Minx moved no faster for him, although her head was up and her ears were pricked. Alec wondered if her lack of interest and response was due to his not wearing silks. He had on boots and breeches but not his silk blouse or cap. It was too hot to wear those. Besides, both he and Henry had decided they weren't fooling Black Minx. She knew the difference between a workout and a race. She just liked the crowd, any crowd.

"So get along with you," Alec pleaded more sharply. "What's ailing you today? They're all watching from the stands. So is Henry. It's not going to be nice when we get back if you don't show a little more go than this."

They were approaching the eight-furlong pole. Here he was supposed to *"Break her off sharp and let her go against the bit"* for the rest of the distance. All the way home, a half-mile in fifty-two seconds. Even old Napoleon could make it in that time.

"Come on, Baby. Come on."

But she wouldn't even take the bit, much less go against it

as Henry had ordered. Alec swung his whip, slapping it hard against his riding boot. It made a lot of noise but it didn't wake the filly up. And that was the only reason he'd carried the whip. She would have stopped completely if it had accidentally touched her.

Actually she was wide awake. The trouble with her today, Alec concluded, was that she didn't *care*. Even the crowd, this record-breaking, shattering, tremendous holiday crowd held no interest for her. It was embarrassing, rounding the far turn and coming down the homestretch in such a slow and easy gallop—especially when the newspapers had announced, "Black Minx will work a half-mile between races, showing Suburban Day patrons some of the speed that won her the Kentucky Derby!"

The spectators didn't exactly boo when the filly galloped past the stands but they didn't applaud either. They were pretty quiet except for a ripple of laughter near the end. Alec thought he heard someone shout, "Get a horse, Ramsay!" But he wasn't sure.

He didn't have any trouble complying with Henry's final order, *"Don't pull her up too sharp. . . . Ease her off easy, nice and easy."*

The big job was to keep her going until they'd reached the barn gate. She hadn't gone faster than the fifty-two seconds Henry had stipulated either. Her time was probably closer to one hundred and two. Well, Henry hadn't set any limit on how slow they could go, had he?

At the barn gate Alec slipped off the filly and looked at her for many long seconds before taking her down the dirt lane. It wasn't the first time he'd seen a horse go "track sour" but never had he seen one sour as completely as this. She was so disinterested in everything about her that she actually *looked* bored. They'd better send her home to get over it.

Later Henry agreed with Alec about sending Black Minx back to the farm but he said it in a few thousand words. It was only in the cool of the night while they sat with Don Conover in his living room that Alec suggested an alternative before putting Black Minx in the van.

"Don," he said, "the way Wintertime's acting you're in the same fix we are. You'll never have him ready for the Belmont."

"Not if I can't work him," Conover agreed. "And I don't believe in working a horse when he leaves grain in his box. Something's wrong but the vet can't find out what it is. He needs to be turned out, I guess. Let him chew on some grass a month or so, then maybe— Say, how about boarding him at your place?"

"Why not?" Henry asked. "We got the room, and the way things seem to be goin' we'll need the money we get for it."

Alec said, "Neither of you have let me finish."

"Go ahead then," Conover said jokingly, "Dr. Ramsay."

"I've had an idea right along that your colt and our filly—"

"Oh, *no*, Alec," Henry interrupted, rising from the couch. He went to the door but didn't leave the room. He just stood there, waiting and shaking his head.

Alec's gaze returned to Don Conover, who was closer to his age than Henry's. "I'm not going to ask much," he said, "—only that we stable the colt and filly next to each other. Also, I'd like to see them worked *together* again."

"Y'mean like we did down at Pimlico?" Conover asked.

"Yes."

"Aren't you afraid she'll quit on you like she did then?" the young trainer asked.

"She won't if your colt keeps going," Alec answered without looking at Henry.

Don Conover shrugged his shoulders. "I don't get you, Alec, but I'm sure willing to try it. I'd try anything to get my colt back on his feed in time for the Belmont."

There was a loud snort as the door opened and closed behind Henry.

Early the next morning Black Minx was moved to the other side of the barn and by nightfall Wintertime had cleaned up all the grain in his three feedings. The filly had always eaten well but now there was a marked change in her in other ways. She suddenly began taking an interest in the activity going on outside her stall instead of sulking in back as she'd done. She whinnied at the stablemen all day long and once grabbed Billy Watts's arm. She nipped him, giving him a scare, but didn't take hold.

That night Henry decided it had been too quiet for her on the other side of the barn. She liked having people around. Maybe Alec had something, at that. Moving her over where more fuss was going on might renew her interest in racing again. It might at that. At least it was worth a try.

Alec decided that the difference in Black Minx was not due just to a change in her surroundings. It was not as simple as that by any means. Actually they were practicing an amateurish form of psychological therapy on Black Minx. If being where she could see Wintertime was going to make her into a racehorse again, he was all for it. But what they were getting into he didn't know. He was no doctor.

"Go ahead and laugh," he told Henry, "but you've always maintained that a contented mind in a healthy body is just as applicable to horses as to humans. So it's not very funny when we happen to own a horse with a mental quirk, even if you don't want to label it 'love.' "

Don Conover decided that he didn't care what was responsible for his colt's improvement. It was enough that he could get him onto the track again and have him ready for the Belmont.

But none of the three expected the sensational workouts of the following week when they put the two horses on the track together.

In the gray early light of dawn Black Minx gave Alec Ramsay rides such as few jockeys were privileged to take at that hour of the day. Billy Watts was one of the "privileged few," for morning after morning Wintertime bobbed head to head, eye to eye with the black filly.

Trainer Don Conover, of Parkslope Stables, remarked to trainer Henry Dailey, of Hopeful Farm, while sitting high in the vast empty stands the morning before the running of the historic Belmont Stakes, "It's hard to believe even when I see them go." He glanced at his stopwatch. "And I can't even believe this. If you tell anyone what they just worked that half-mile in, I'll say it's a lie."

Trainer Henry Dailey answered, "One thing sure is that their two heads will be bobbin' as one again tomorrow. Whatever we get out of this race, we'll get together."

Trainer Don Conover shrugged his big shoulders. He didn't understand that part of it. He just knew that he had Wintertime as sharp as he could get him and that was razor sharp. He figured, too, that over the Belmont distance of a mile and a half his colt had the stamina to pull ahead of the filly. Actually he wasn't worried about beating *her*. There was only one horse to beat in the stretch run and that was Eclipse. Everybody knew that—*everybody*.

The Belmont

13

There were two television sets upstairs in the jockeys' room at Belmont Park, and they were usually on at the same time. One was a closed-circuit set showing only the races as they were run on the track below. The other was a standard set carrying, among other things, baseball.

For the jockeys who did not have mounts in the sixth race, Saturday afternoon, June 12, was no different from any other day. The larger group was watching the Mets play the Phillies at Shea Stadium. Then someone at the closed-circuit set said, "It's on. Pick it up on yours and we'll get the whole works, even the commercials."

Michael Costello, who had ridden in the fifth race and was done for the day, switched channels and there were no dissenters among the baseball fans. Instead everyone moved closer to the set to make room for others and there was a colorful merging of rich silks.

The picture on the screen showed the track below and the infield. "Welcome, ladies and gentlemen," the announcer said, "to Belmont Park where within a few minutes we'll witness the running of the historic Belmont Stakes, the third leg of America's Triple Crown for three-year-old colts and fillies."

A valet watching said, "At least it ain't so awful hot like it was Memorial Day. At least it ain't that bad." He was stripped to the waist and wore a canvas apron. Perspiration rolled from his naked chest while he polished a shining black boot.

"What's the heat got to do with it, anyway?" another valet asked. "They run the same, hot or cold."

"I wasn't thinkin' of them," the first valet answered. "It was *those* poor guys I was thinkin' about, that's all."

The picture showed the flat, uncovered roof of the long stands where people sat exposed to a glowing sun. Then the cameras swept down to the packed crowd standing between the track and grandstand.

"They knew what kind of a mob would be here today," the second valet said unkindly. "I don't feel sorry for them one bit. I'm just glad I don't have to be out there."

"Quit arguin'," a jockey said, "or we'll *put* you there."

The picture shifted to Belmont's soft green lawns behind the stands where some fans sat on benches under old and towering shade trees while others could be seen walking about.

"There," a jockey said to the chastened valet. "Does that make you feel better? Plenty of room. Good ol' Belmont, spacious Belmont. Plenty of room for everybody, on the track and off."

"At least it ain't a madhouse like Churchill Downs on Derby Day!" someone said defiantly.

"Heaven forbid!" another answered mockingly. "Our checkered waistcoat boys wouldn't allow anything like that, not *at dear old Belmont!*"

"But we got a band to class up the big one today. They went that far anyway," a jockey in the back remarked.

"But it's not like Pimlico's band," another rider said. "Pimlico puts on the best show, all right. I mean it. You jus' shoulda heard that band play on Preakness Day. It would have torn your heart out. I'm tellin' you it would."

"Stop crying," a jockey on the outside of the group said, "and turn up the sound so we can hear something. Think we just want to stand around looking at pictures? We can go outside if we just want to *see*. Let's listen to what this guy has to say."

They were suddenly quiet, not because of the jockey's request but because the horses had come onto the track.

". . . and so, ladies and gentlemen, this is the Belmont," the announcer said, "called by many horsemen 'the test of the champion' and rightly so, for it is raced over the true English Derby distance of a mile and a half. Even more than the Kentucky Derby and the Preakness this historic race requires stamina as well as speed."

The jockeys in the room listened in respectful silence, some with awe on their faces and others with sheer envy. Suddenly the quiet was broken as the screen showed a close-up of a horse wearing the number 1 saddle cloth.

"There's Pops!" several riders yelled together.

Big and brown and burly with splashes of white on his face and legs, Eclipse broke from the post parade and can-tered past the stands. His stable pony had trouble keeping up with him even at that slow gait for his strides were enormous.

An apprentice jockey, moving closer to the screen, said, "The strip's dryin' out after last night's rain. It'll be good if not fast. Look at it."

"Naw," another said, "see those light brown patches? Well, they're just baked on top. It's wet underneath and bad goin'. This track's got too much top soil to dry out in anything less than *days*."

"Hey! Don't I hear the band playin' 'Sidewalks of New York'?" a valet asked. "Where they got them hid anyway?"

"Behind the stands," and someone laughed, "so no one can see 'em! But let's listen to what this guy's sayin', huh?"

They knew Eclipse far better than the announcer did but they listened attentively. He made it real easy for folks to know what kind of horse they were looking at. They could just see the millions of people at home, sitting in their armchairs and listening to this guy talk about Pops. They just could.

"Eclipse is the heavy favorite and must be considered the champion to be tested in this classic race. According to those who know him best he will not be found wanting today. In fact they have already placed the very positive adjective *great* on his broad, flat back."

A jockey said, "Broad is right. I swear y'could set a table for six on it."

"Quiet!"

"Okay, okay."

". . . and most horsemen," the television announcer continued, "discount Eclipse's loss to Black Minx in the Kentucky Derby since the big brown colt hadn't yet found himself. This is not the same horse, they say, who was beaten in the Derby."

"But she whipped him good," a rider said. "Baby really did it, no matter what this guy says about Pops not being the same horse in the Derby. And that was a big one, too, a real big one. Maybe even the biggest no matter what this guy says about the Belmont bein' a test of champions or somethin'."

"He just meant that it separates the sprinters from the stayers, that's all," a valet explained patiently.

"Well, maybe so," the jockey answered, "but the Derby ain't no sprint. Baby can stay with the best of them, Baby can."

"Keep quiet, will ya?"

"All right, all right . . ."

The cameras were still on Eclipse while he slowed to a walk.

"After the Kentucky Derby," the announcer continued, "Eclipse set a new world record in the Withers Mile here at Belmont and then, of course, went down to Pimlico to defeat his Derby conqueror. Most impressive while winning the Preakness was his equaling the track record over a very muddy strip. The big colt can handle wet footing such as he has again today but his long strides aren't best suited for it. Eclipse will, of course, be ridden by his regular rider, the young veteran Ted Robinson."

The picture shifted to Wintertime, the second horse in the post parade. The blood bay colt went into a lope before the stands, his strides coming short but very confident.

"Now here's a colt who seems to delight in this wet kind of going," the announcer told his television audience. "Wintertime has run some of his best races here at Belmont Park, which is his home track. Some people figure that he just might be the horse Eclipse will have to catch in the stretch run. He finished second in the Kentucky Derby and tied for third with Black Minx in the Preakness. Perhaps this will be *his* day, the day he stops being best man and becomes the groom. . . ."

"What a silly way to talk about a horse," a jockey commented. "What's he mean anyway?"

"Just that Red's due to win one, that's all," came the answer.

"Then what's he been building up Pops for? He just got through telling everybody that Pops was the champ, didn't he?"

"He's got to make it sound like a tough race for Pops," the other answered. "It's his job, that's what it is. He's only got four other horses out there. He's got to make people think Pops is really doin' something in beatin' 'em."

"He hasn't beaten them yet," another rider said quietly.

The cameras were shifting to Golden Vanity, the third horse in the post parade, when Black Minx whipped out of line and came down the center of the track. The cameras remained on her as she swept by Golden Vanity while trying to break away from her stable pony and rider.

"There's the Kentucky Derby winner," the announcer said quickly. "Number five, Black Minx. She seems peppery today and full of run. There, now they have her stopped. But she's not going to be led back to last position in the parade. She's going to stay up there alongside Wintertime. They're letting her, so everything seems to be under control now. Alec Ramsay is sitting back in his saddle. That's Henry Dailey, Hopeful Farm's trainer, acting as pony boy. He had his hands full for a few seconds there.

"Black Minx may surprise everyone by going out in front and staying there today," the announcer confided to his audience. "Fillies aren't supposed to win Belmonts any more than Kentucky Derbies but apparently no one's told Black Minx. She may be the only filly since Ruthless in 1867 to win the Belmont Stakes. Remember, too, she's carrying the same weight as she did in the Kentucky Derby. That's one hundred and twenty-one pounds. The colts give five pounds to a filly in this long run of a mile and a half, carrying one hundred twenty-six."

A jockey said, "There he goes again, makin' it sound like a tough one for Pops."

"Listen, Mac," another rider said, "this guy knows that after today he's not goin' to have any three-year-olds to talk about *except* Pops. There aren't goin' to be any trainers willing to send their colts out against him, that's what! It would be too humiliating, and trainers and owners don't like to be humiliated before thousands of people. Pops will have the rest of the three-year-old races to himself. They'll be 'walkovers' for him."

A few minutes later the horses were entering the starting gate and the jockeys' room, like the stands outside, became very quiet.

Eclipse walked quickly into his number 1 stall and stood there, waiting. Wintertime balked behind his stall and shook his hooded head angrily. A ground crewman took him by the bridle and led him inside. Golden Vanity went willingly enough into the number 3 stall but kept going and broke through the closed front flaps. An outrider was there to pick him up and he didn't get away. He was taken around the gate and inside again. This time he stayed. Silver Jet stood quietly in the number 4 stall, making no more fuss than Eclipse. Black Minx refused to go into her box, rearing and throwing herself sideways. It took two assistant starters to get her into the number 5 stall. They stayed there holding her, while she let fly her hind legs at the padded door to her rear.

Now there were mumbled mutterings from the tense jockeys in the room. Any second and the door flaps would be opened. They knew it as well as if they'd been in the gate themselves.

"No chance. No chance," one said. "Red's up in the air." Wintertime had reared and Billy Watts was having trouble getting him down.

"Keep quiet. You ain't out there."

"Look at Pops, will you?" another rider said. "He looks bored. I mean it."

"He looks lopsided to me," someone answered.

"Lopsided nothin'. Wait'll you see him come out. Straight as a die."

"Quiet!" Michael Costello bellowed. " 'Tis the announcer I'll be a-listenin' to and not to the likes of any of you!"

"Eclipse is usually a slow starter," the announcer said quietly while waiting for Wintertime to stop rearing. "He takes a while to get in stride but the long race is all in his favor, especially the quarter-of-a-mile homestretch."

"What's he talking about?" a jockey asked. "Pops breaks fast, *then* falls back because he wants to race that way. He likes to bowl 'em over in the stretch run, that's what Pops does."

The stall doors suddenly burst open and the horses came plunging out of the gate. Now the watching jockeys were quiet but their hands and shoulders worked in rhythm with their favorites on the screen.

"Come on, Baby. Come on. Keep her goin', Alec. Push her."

Black Minx must have been in motion just as the starter touched the electric button opening for stall doors, for she came out a stride ahead of the others. Apparently out of control, she lunged in toward the rail but no horse was on her left so she wasn't interfering with anyone. Alec straightened her out skillfully and then took her gently over to the inner rail.

" 'Tis a pretty piece of ridin'," Mike Costello muttered.

"Come on, Baby, keep goin'!" another jockey shouted.

Black Minx began shortening stride or perhaps Alec was taking up a wrap on her. The jockeys watching the screen couldn't tell. But now the rest of the field had caught her. Wintertime had been the next fastest out of the gate and he was the first to reach Black Minx, with Eclipse hard on his heels.

They saw the filly swerve to the right, shaking her head and fighting Alec Ramsay once more. Wintertime slipped into the opening on the rail with Billy Watts hand-riding vigorously.

"Billy's opening up," a valet said. "He's not goin' to sit behind any horses today."

"Neither is Ted!" someone shouted from in back of the room.

It was true. Eclipse was moving up alongside Wintertime.

" 'Tis no head start Pops will be givin' the others today!" Mike Costello exclaimed.

Black Minx picked up stride when Wintertime suddenly appeared on her left. She leveled out faster going past the stands, and the crowd roared. Wintertime couldn't pull away from her and Eclipse was staying just behind them!

"She'll last. She's got speed *and* class, that Baby. Come on, Baby!" a jockey said.

"They'll stagger in, both of 'em," another remarked.

"Then so will Pops," someone added. "He ain't droppin' back like he usually does. He's goin' with them!"

Silver Jet and Golden Vanity were three lengths behind, their jockeys a little worried about the others but content to wait until they were on the backstretch before making their moves.

They swept into the first big bend with Billy Watts still pumping Wintertime. But the blood bay colt couldn't pull away from the black filly at his side. Alec Ramsay sat quietly in the saddle, apparently not yet ready to ask more of his mount.

Ted Robinson sat just as still as Alec, and Eclipse wasn't losing any ground to the speedy front runners. The brown colt's strides seemed to be twice the length of the leaders' and suddenly his big body blocked out the screen's view of them.

"That's all there is to this race!" a valet shouted.

The picture shifted and they could see the horses sweeping around the long turn with no change in positions. Going down the backstretch Silver Jet and Golden Vanity made their moves but they couldn't quite catch the three leaders. Their jockeys took up on them again, apparently deciding to wait until the run for home before trying once more.

"It's smart to wait," someone in the room said. "You'd think Alec would take back too. He's smart enough to know he and Billy are killing each other off."

"What about Pops? He's still there, ain't he? Ain't you worried about him killin' himself off?"

"Pops is running well within himself," came the answer.

"No he's not," another argued. "Look at Ted. His hands are down. He's asking for speed."

"If he's asking and that's all he's getting, Pops isn't the horse he's cracked up to be," someone shouted. There was a nodding of heads in complete agreement.

All eyes were now on Eclipse as the field neared the far turn. Here would come the test of greatness. There was still a half-mile to go. Would Eclipse stagger home, fighting off the others to the finish, or would he win like the champion he was supposed to be? Was it to be a finish between Wintertime and Black Minx with Eclipse out of it? Or would the trailing Golden Vanity and Silver Jet come up with conserved stamina to win?

They were past the sweeping turn and on the straightaway when suddenly, to the loud shouts of the viewers, Eclipse came around the two leaders in mighty leaps! Ted Robinson tapped him once with his whip and the big colt started drawing away as if the others were standing still. The viewers saw Alec Ramsay lower his hands, urging his filly to accept Eclipse's challenge. But Black Minx wouldn't budge for him. She stayed with Wintertime, stride for stride.

Billy Watts had given Wintertime a breather but now he went at him again, using hands, whip and feet in a final effort to catch Eclipse. His urging was futile, for the long-striding leader pulled ever farther away. Soon all that appeared on the television screen was a big brown colt running all by himself down the long homestretch. Twice Robinson looked back and finally he stopped asking Eclipse for any more speed. He was sitting quietly in his saddle when his mount swept under the wire.

"Now let's get back to the race," a jockey said mockingly as the cameras swept over the distance between the winner and the rest of the field.

The picture showed the oncoming horses. Golden Vanity was in front with Silver Jet a length behind him. Far to the rear were Wintertime and Black Minx.

"Looks like Billy's pullin' up!" someone said excitedly. "Red's hurt. The left fore. He's limping. See? He wants to come on but Billy won't let him. He's stoppin' him."

"Yeah," another agreed, "but why don't Baby come on? What's wrong with her anyway? She's not hurt but she ain't comin' on!"

Not until Wintertime came to a dead stop was Alec Ramsay able to get Black Minx past the colt. The viewers watched while she finished the race at a slow gallop, shaking her head all the way.

"She's just a sprinter," a valet said disappointedly, "and all the time I thought she had *class*."

" 'Tis not the truth ye speak," Mike Costello said quietly. "Ye don't win the Kentucky Derby on speed alone. No, me boy, there's something else that's a-troublin' her."

The Parkslope Stables' barn was very quiet after the running of the Belmont Stakes. Jean Parshall, Wintertime's owner, was in the colt's stall. So was Don Conover, his trainer, and Billy Watts, his jockey, and old Ray Jenkins, his groom. With them was their veterinarian.

Alec and Henry watched, along with others, from outside the stall, their eyes as concerned as everyone else's.

"You got someone walkin' the filly?" Henry whispered to Alec.

Alec nodded. "Mike Costello came around and offered to help."

The blanketed colt stood quietly in his stall. Mingled with his sweat was the sharp odor of medication. His left foreleg had already filled and was hot to the touch. He held his hoof off the straw bedding.

They all knew that the tendons between the knee and ankle joint had been severely strained. Bowed tendons weren't uncommon in horses working at high speed. A slip or a blow could do it. The injured horse rarely was able to equal his best previous efforts. Whether or not he ever raced at all depended upon how severely the tendon tissue had been ruptured.

"How bad is it, Doctor?" Jean Parshall asked gravely.

The veterinarian shook his head. "You'd better not figure on racing him again, Miss Parshall."

The young woman turned and left the stall.

"Don't take it so hard, Jean," Henry said kindly when she came up to him. "He's done more than most horses do in a whole lifetime."

"I know, Henry," she said without looking at the trainer. "It's just that . . . well, he was such a game little horse. He never quit trying, even against the big ones when everyone knew darn well he was beaten. He was going after Eclipse when it happened. I saw him slip coming off the turn."

Don Conover came out of the stall and stood with them. "He'll make a good stallion for some farm, Jean," he said quietly. "Look at it that way. It's the horse business. We'll get a good price for him and—"

She shook her head. "I don't care about the money," she interrupted. "I want a good home for him. It's the only time I've ever regretted not having a stock farm."

Henry said, "Would you let him go for twenty thousand dollars, Jean?"

Alec turned quickly to his friend. They didn't need another stallion and twenty thousand was just about all they'd made toward the new barn! Getting the filly to finish the Belmont had earned them fourth place and a purse of $5,000.

"I know you could get more," Henry added, "but you said you wanted a good home for him. That's all we can afford to pay."

Alec watched Jean Parshall turn to her trainer and then saw them both nod their heads in assent. Alec's gaze shifted to the ring where Black Minx was being walked by Mike Costello. He realized then that she, too, was going home. Her racing days, like Wintertime's, were over. Henry had made all the arrangements.

Later the trainer said, "I guess I'm an old fool, Alec, but we'll send them back together. That's the way she's wanted it all along."

"You don't sound so old, Henry," Alec answered quietly.

And More Speed!

14

Only the afternoons were different during the days that followed. The spring meeting at Belmont Park closed with the running of the Belmont Stakes and then came the opening of nearby Aqueduct Race Course. The great stands at Belmont were empty and silent but the stable area remained unchanged, for most of the horses stayed at Belmont and went to Aqueduct only to race.

Alec watched a long horse van being loaded one afternoon. "Couldn't Aqueduct run its programs on its own stabling area?" he asked Henry.

"It's not so big," the trainer said. "They'd find it pretty difficult, I guess. Anyway, what's a half-hour ride when we're comfortably settled here?"

Alec left his seat on the barn bench to go to the paddock where Peek-a-Boo grazed beneath a shade tree. Yes, it was easy to remain at Belmont Park and be content. He ran a hand under the Shetland pony's heavy forelock, trying to comfort her in Wintertime's absence. The blood bay colt had been sent to the farm with Black Minx that morning.

Henry joined Alec at the fence. "To look at you you'd think Black Minx had it real tough bein' sent home," the trainer said.

Alec smiled. "I don't mean to look that way. I guess I just feel awfully disappointed in her."

"She got beat by Eclipse," Henry said quietly. "That's the best excuse a horse could have."

"She had the speed to go after him," Alec answered. "She was going nice and easy coming off the turn, then Wintertime slipped and that was when he bowed the tendon. When Billy began pulling him up she went all to pieces. I had an awful time getting her to finish the race."

"She's a top filly," Henry said, "but she's no Black. She's got her mind on other things besides racing. Horses got to *feel* like racing to race well. They've got to be happy at it. If they're unhappy and you can't help them, you'd better just forget them for a while."

"She felt like running in the Derby," Alec reminded him.

Henry nodded. "That was *her* race, Alec. She wanted to run that day and she was the best three-year-old in training at the time."

"But you don't think she could have caught Eclipse on Saturday even if she'd been at her very best?"

"No, I don't," Henry said. "As far as Eclipse is concerned Black Minx had better stick with the fillies. He's a great horse, Alec. Mark my words. Someday soon I want you to stand off where you can see him race. You've been ridin' behind him too much. You've lost your perspective."

Alec grinned. "I've got to admit that I haven't seen much

beside his hindquarters—and they're pretty powerful ones at that."

"Eclipse really turned on the speed in the Belmont," Henry said. "He really did. He stayed with you and Billy Watts when you were sprintin' your fool heads off, and then he smothered you with a still faster burst of speed comin' around the bend, and he *stayed*. I wish you could have seen it. I wish you could."

"I was busy," Alec said.

"He moved so easily and swiftly that it was hard to believe even when you *did* see it," Henry went on. "Yep, he sure made an army of new fans Saturday. They saw a race to tell their kiddies about when they got home."

Alec said, "It was an easy way to pick up eighty-two thousand dollars, all right. In fact, we didn't have to work awfully hard for our five."

"No, we didn't," Henry agreed, "seein' we only had an injured horse to beat."

Henry turned away from the fence and Alec followed him.

"I guess you're still sore at me for buyin' Red," the trainer said.

"I wasn't sore before so why should I be sore now?" Alec asked. "You handle our money, so if that's what you thought best to do with it, why—"

"Aw, Alec, you *know* I feel the new barn's more important than another colt. It was just . . . well, you know how it is . . . anyway, if I had to do it over again I wouldn't do it."

Alec put his hand on the old man's arm. "Sure you would, Henry. You know darn well you would."

They walked the rest of the way to the barn in silence. As

they reached the door Henry said, "Well, it just takes one big purse to build it, anyway."

"I'm not worrying about the new barn," Alec answered confidently. "The Black is sharp and full of run. He'll make the money for us in a couple of jumps."

"It won't be *quite* that easy," Henry cautioned. "Remember he's goin' to have to cope with Casey *and* a lot of weight on his back."

Alec grinned. "Then it'll take us a little longer. A few more jumps, a few more races."

Henry nodded his big head. "I guess so. I can't see us *not* makin' enough money to pay for the new barn, not these days with the purses so high. Just as long as he stays sound—"

"Don't even think he won't," Alec interrupted gravely.

"I'm not thinkin' it. I just happened to say it."

"Don't even say it," Alec begged him. "We're down to a one-horse stable—a big horse, but still just one horse. If anything happens to him we can't go anywhere but home."

The next morning Alec, wearing a T-shirt and jeans, rode the Black onto Belmont's training track. Its surface of sandy loam was more like that of the Aqueduct strip than the main track. The sun wasn't up yet and the air felt cool on Alec's bare arms. It was exhilarating to be out so early and he was as eager to run as the big horse beneath him. Holding the Black would be a difficult job this morning.

Henry rode Napoleon beside them. "Don Conover wants us to push that bay gelding of his," the trainer said. He wasn't looking at Alec but at the Black's hoofs. "I thought he missed a step back there," he added nervously.

"Stop worrying," Alec said. "There's nothing wrong with

him. I'd feel him give way if there was." He noticed the winter jacket Henry wore and the rubbers on his feet even though the ground was dry. Henry was being very careful of himself these days, almost too careful. "How far does Don want us to go with him?" Alec asked.

"Six furlongs," the trainer answered, his eyes still following the Black's strides. "But maybe we shouldn't, Alec. He just *might* have taken a misstep back there. We can't be too careful. You know as well as I do what the stakes are."

The stallion almost jumped from under Alec before he had a chance to answer Henry. He waited until he had him back in a walk again before saying, "If we can't work him, we can't race him."

The trainer nodded thoughtfully. "Will you be able to hold him back?" he finally asked. "Don thinks his horse would like to feel he's winning. He's raced second to Casey the last three times out."

"I'll hold him," Alec promised.

"Go around once with me," Henry ordered, pulling the shank between them.

The Black bowed his neck against Alec's snug hold but he didn't shake his head or try to break away. He loped along easily beside old Napoleon.

Henry watched him all the way around. There was no evidence of a misstep in the Black's strides. "I guess I was wrong," he told Alec. "But you got me worryin' so, talkin' like you did about us bein' down to a *one-horse stable*."

"I'm sorry I ever mentioned it. Anyway, he's as sound as they come so you don't have to worry."

"Oh, I'll worry all right," Henry answered quietly. "I always worry."

Don Conover was waiting for them with Gunfire, a bay gelding. Alec knew him to be a fast handicap horse who'd won a great deal of money for the Parkslope Stables. When this horse was good he was very good indeed and it took Casey to beat him.

Don Conover said, "I appreciate this, Henry. He needs to be pushed hard and I don't have anything in the stable to push him with." His gaze shifted to Alec. "But I don't want you to catch him. I think if he gets his head in front and finds he can keep it there it'll mean a big difference in his next race."

Alec nodded. "Sure, Don," he said. "We'll keep close but behind."

The young trainer's eyes turned to the Black. "I hate to make a workhorse of him."

"Stop talkin' and let's go!" Henry said impatiently. "I haven't had coffee yet."

The exercise boy riding Gunfire took him into the first turn at a gallop. Alec waited until the gelding was some ten lengths beyond and then sent the Black after him.

For the moment the track was clear except for the two working horses. The Black's eyes and ears followed the horse ahead of him as he bent into the turn. Alec kept him at a gallop. Both horses were to break into a run at the six-furlong pole, which was just off the first turn going into the backstretch.

"Easy, Black," Alec said. "Easy." He was standing in his stirrups, doing his best not to close the gap too fast between the two horses.

At the six-furlong pole the gelding broke into a hard run and the Black, too, leaped forward, taking hold of the bit. Alec sat back in his saddle, the wind whistling in his ears. As both horses began settling into their strides, the long back-stretch lay before them.

Alec took the bit from the Black and kept him under a snug hold. Gunfire was using his top speed early and was holding on to his long lead. Alec let out a wrap of the reins. Don wanted his horse pushed and they weren't pushing by staying so far behind.

The Black's speed came with a burst as if all his pent-up energy had been released at once. Swiftly the gap between the two horses closed and as they swept into the far turn Alec took up on the Black again. For a few strides the stallion shook his head in his eagerness to go on. Alec took up another wrap of the reins and the Black slowed obediently.

The gelding was leveled out two lengths beyond. His long ears were flicked backward as though he'd actually been listening to the Black coming up on him. His strides came faster as he pounded into the homestretch. He began pulling away.

When Gunfire was good he was awfully good, Alec reminded himself, and he was good today!

Alec felt the Black reach for the bit again as he sent him after Gunfire. He kept it from him but the stallion surged forward with mighty leaps. The gelding took up the challenge and fought him off furiously.

The last furlong pole flashed by, and for a second Alec forgot his instructions in the boiling heat of the stretch run. The leather slid through his wet hands and eagerly the Black took advantage of the extra rein, drawing alongside the gelding in one jump. Then Alec caught a glimpse of Henry and Don far down the track, seated astride their stable ponies. Quickly he took up rein. The Black shook his head furiously and his teeth sought the bit again. Alec kept it from him and the gelding was in front as the horses swept beneath the finish wire.

When Alec had slowed the Black and was turning him at a walk, Henry rode up and said gravely, "Get off, Alec. I think he missed a step in that left foreleg."

All the way back to the barn they watched the Black's strides carefully and found nothing wrong.

"Still, I want to make sure," Henry said. "I'll call the vet."

"Let's not look too hard for trouble, Henry," Alec pleaded. "As long as he cools out all right, I don't see any reason for a vet."

But Henry had his way. The next morning, even though the Black's legs and hoofs were cool to the touch and he walked soundly, Henry had Alec pull off all four shoes. The veterinarian found nothing wrong but Henry insisted upon his taking X-rays. These, too, disclosed no injury anywhere.

"I hope you're satisfied now, Henry," the veterinarian said. "I've never known anyone to do so much worrying before we found anything wrong."

"We've got a big stake in this horse, Doc," Henry answered.

"Worrying isn't going to help any."

Regardless of the veterinarian's sound advice Henry didn't work the Black during the next few days for fear his legs would be hurt in some way. By the end of the week the stallion was almost bursting with energy and eager for much more than his walks about the stable area. His legs were as sound as they'd ever been in his life, Alec knew. But Henry's orders remained the same and Alec and the Black walked and walked.

On one of their trips they came upon Michael Costello grazing Casey. The chestnut's head jerked up fast when the

Black approached. Alec tightened the lead shank and his horse swung around.

He was about to leave when Mike asked, "Did ye hear the nerve of that upstart Pops?"

Alec shook his head. Eclipse was one of the few horses who had been moved to Aqueduct right after his victory in the Belmont.

" 'Tis a-steppin' out of his class he is on Saturday in the Summer Festival Handicap," Mike said.

Alec's face showed his great surprise. It wasn't often that a three-year-old left his age group to race older competition. Not even the great colt Man o' War had gone into the open handicaps.

"Aren't you and Casey scheduled to go in that race too?" he asked.

Michael Costello's black eyes flashed. " 'Tis the truth ye speak, and I'm a-promisin' that Casey will be puttin' the youngster in his place."

Later Alec told Henry what Mike had said and the trainer chuckled. "I'll believe such a lickin' when I see it. Mike will have his hands full and Casey had better be at his Saturday best. Pops is sharp after the Belmont and no one's told *him* that the horses he'll be racin' are older and more experienced. He's used to winning and he's big and strong enough to handle all of them, including Casey."

The following Saturday Alec and Henry were among the great crowd at Aqueduct who watched Eclipse go to the post against ten of the best handicap stars in the country. Casey, however, wasn't one of them. He had not cleaned his feed-box that morning and his trainer was taking no chances of hurting his champion with the much richer Carter and Brooklyn Handicaps only a few weeks off.

The announcement of Casey's withdrawal from the race was greeted by a loud clamor of disapproval. It was the lure of a meeting between Eclipse and Casey that had swelled the stands. For a long while the booing continued. *Was the great Casey scared of the three-year-old champion?* the fans asked themselves. *Was that the real reason he'd been scratched from the race?*

Henry shook his head in disgust at the clamor. He would have liked to tell those people a thing or two. One Saturday they applauded a horse to the skies for a superior race and the next Saturday they ran him into the ground. He would have liked to expose their ignorance. A trainer didn't race a horse who wasn't a hundred percent well. Would they rather have seen Casey run a mediocre race and be beaten? Was that what they wanted? Didn't they care that he might be hurt for life and ruin his whole career? All for a Saturday race that didn't amount to much more than a seven-furlong workout for such a horse?

"The race you want will come off," he muttered. *"You'll see it when they're both ready to go at the same time, and it'll be for keeps."*

"What'd you say, Henry?" Alec asked.

"Nothin' . . . except, well—" the old trainer's eyes were on the horses entering the gate, "I was thinkin' that it wasn't fair to Pops to make him give pounds as well as years in his first race against older horses."

With Casey out of the race, Eclipse was carrying top weight of 126 pounds, 10 less than Casey would have carried if he'd gone to the post but 5 pounds more than any other horse in the present field.

Alec watched Don Conover's Gunfire with whom the Black had worked a few days ago. The bay gelding was the second heaviest-weighted horse, carrying 121 pounds. Billy Watts was up on him.

"The crowd seems to agree with the handicapper," Alec said. "They've made Eclipse a heavy favorite even at the weight and age concession."

Henry grunted, "We'll know in a minute who's right."

The answer came swiftly and conclusively. As soon as Eclipse left the starting gate and before his jockey could hold him back after a fast break, he sprinted through a hole between two inside horses, brushing the rail in his eagerness to get out in front. After a few long strides he surged ahead of Gunfire and then everybody saw that there was no holding him back.

For the first time in his life, Eclipse took the lead early in a race. There was nothing his jockey, Ted Robinson, could do about it except to try to rate the colt's speed, hoping to save enough to meet any challenge that might come from behind in the homestretch.

Alec saw Robinson take a new hold on the reins but there was no shortening of Eclipse's strides. Instead the burly colt drew ever farther away from the rest of the field. Alec knew then that Eclipse had gripped the bit, that he was running the way the Black had raced in the Speed Handicap.

Eclipse swept around Aqueduct's sharp far turn and came thundering down the homestretch. Nobody among the great crowd expected to see any horse from the field come running at him and none did. His extreme speed had smothered them all and as the older handicap stars began fading still farther in the distance even the most conservative horsemen watching knew that here was one of the fastest horses of all time.

In silent homage they watched Eclipse sweep under the

wire all by himself. They broke into an ever-swelling roar only when the electric lights flashed the time of the seven-furlong race on the center-field board.

Eclipse had shattered the Black's record set in the Speed Handicap at Belmont only a few weeks before!

Skyrocket

15

The policeman on the corner waved as Alec crossed the street and, entering the drugstore, the boy heard someone say, "There goes Ramsay." It never used to be like that. He could have walked all over town without anyone's recognizing him. The Black had changed all that for him and for Henry.

It was the middle of a hot afternoon and the soda-fountain counter was crowded with customers eating plates of ice cream topped with thick syrup, whipped cream and nuts. Alec hadn't had lunch and he thought how good a chocolate soda would have tasted. But he resisted the temptation to order it. One didn't get used to eating such delicacies and stay in his business for very long. Not that weight had ever been too big a worry with him.

He found an empty stool. "A hamburger, please," he told the counterman, "with lettuce and tomato."

"You could eat all you want and still make weight on the Black," a voice beside him said.

Turning his head, he saw that Billy Watts was seated on the stool next to him. "Hi, Billy," he said in greeting. "I didn't see you there."

The young jockey lifted the tall malted milk shake in front of him. "You were too busy looking at this," he answered. "Have one on me."

Alec smiled. "If I had one, I'd have another. Then when I couldn't keep away from them, Henry would come up with a light mount for me to ride and I wouldn't be able to make the weight."

"I guess so," Billy Watts admitted, smiling too. "You're better off the stuff."

Alec watched his friend take another long swallow of the milk shake. *Really,* he thought, *Billy should stay away from such rich food.* He was stocky and getting stockier. His broad, cheerful face was getting broader, too, if not more cheerful.

The young jockey set his glass down. "My big worry is something else," he said, his face suddenly very sober.

Alec didn't bother to ask him what it was. He'd seen Billy being crowded going into the first turn in Saturday's race and thought he knew. Billy had been close to going down.

"Red's doing okay," Alec said, changing the subject. "We called home last night. They've got a good vet taking care of his leg."

"Fine, that's fine," Billy said. He finished his milk shake and ordered another.

"You really *are* going to the dogs," Alec said lightly. Billy didn't laugh or say anything in response.

The hamburger came and Alec started eating. Finally he broke the strained silence that had come between them. "They're saying he humiliated the handicapper as well as the rest of you. He took the race too easily."

"Pops, y'mean?"

Alec nodded.

"He made a *hard* one look easy," Billy said earnestly. "No one would have known he was racing some of the best handicap horses in the game. But then again he's no normal three-year-old. He should have given us even more pounds than he did. He's the greatest colt I've ever seen." The milk shake came and he drank half of it before setting the glass down.

Alec nodded. "A good many of the old-timers seem to feel that way too. A lot more of them have climbed on his bandwagon."

"It wasn't even an important race to him," Billy said wonderingly. "Just a tightener for the big-money Dwyer next Saturday. That's all it was."

Alec took another bite of his hamburger and then said, "I don't know why he has to be very tight for that race. It's for his own age group and he has complete domination of that division. If he keeps up the luck he's had so far, it'll take Casey and the Black to beat him."

"That's a race I'd like to see," Billy said. "But I don't think his trainer will go out looking for trouble," he added thoughtfully.

"He would have had it if Casey had raced Saturday."

"Yeah, I guess he would. How is Casey anyway? Was he really sick, do you think?"

"He's not sick now but maybe that's because he didn't

race," Alec answered. "Mike Costello worked him fast this morning. They'll be going in the Carter Handicap next Monday."

"That's the Black's race, too, isn't it?"

"It is if Henry is satisfied with the weight assignments," Alec replied. "He won't let him go if they pack too many pounds on him against a horse like Casey."

"Would a hundred and forty be too much?" Billy asked, finishing his milk shake.

"Sure it would. No horse has carried that much weight in the fifty-odd years the Carter's been run."

"I understand that this year some horse is packing it," Billy said wisely. "*Your* horse."

"You mean—" Alec stopped, studying Billy's round face. There was some chocolate around his lower lip. "How do you know?" he asked finally.

"The weights were announced about an hour ago."

"I was in Flushing," Alec said. "How much did they give Casey?"

"One hundred and thirty-five."

"The Black won't race then," Alec said. "Henry won't let him. He's worried now about his breaking down, and with one hundred and forty pounds on his back—"

"I'm not interested," Billy interrupted abruptly. "It's your business. I just thought I'd tell you." Catching the counterman's attention, he ordered a doughnut.

"You have any *light* horses to race tomorrow?" Alec asked jokingly, but his eyes were critical when he met Billy's.

"Not tomorrow or ever," Billy answered quietly. "I'm through for good. I got scared in that race, I really did. You might as well be the first to know."

"I don't blame you," Alec said just as quietly, "if that's the way it is."

"It is," Billy replied, taking his eyes off Alec's.

"But Don said you were going to ride Gunfire in the Carter."

"I will if he makes me, but that's all then."

"What will you do?"

The young jockey shrugged his shoulders.

"Would you like to work for us?" Alec asked.

"I'm through with racing, I told you," Billy said. "You know it as well as I do."

"I meant at the farm."

Billy looked at Alec and his eyes disclosed his kindled interest. "Doing what?" he asked.

"We have a foaling man's job open."

"You mean the job the guy had who burned down your barn? Take his place?"

"Yes, and you can help break the yearlings."

Billy Watts said eagerly, "Sure, Alec. Sure I would. Thanks. Thanks a lot. I couldn't want anything more."

Returning later to the barn, Alec saw a group of reporters outside the Black's stall. The top screen door was closed and it was apparent that Henry was inside, for the press were addressing their remarks to him.

"The Black is perfectly sound?" one of the reporters asked.

Henry's gruff voice came from the stall. "That's what the vet says but I'm not sure yet. Anyway I'm not taking any chances lettin' him race with a hundred and forty pounds on his back."

"Then he's out of the Carter?"

Henry didn't answer, and Alec pushed his way through

the crowd. They asked questions of him but he directed
them to Henry. "He's the boss," Alec said, opening the stall
door and going inside.

The stallion stood in the rear of his stall and Henry remained at the door. Alec noticed that while the reporters
were marveling at the Black's fine muscles Henry was looking gravely at the left foreleg. Alec decided that Henry was
overdoing his apparent concern for the Black's soundness.
There was no fever in the foreleg and if anything had been
wrong it would have shown up in the morning's run. He'd
worked the stallion alone and fast. The Black had not missed
a step, then or later.

The stallion came to Alec and the boy stroked him while
listening to Henry and the reporters.

"He wouldn't be carrying much more than Casey," a
newsman said. "Only five pounds. Casey's going."

"That's his trainer's business," Henry retorted. "If he
wants to give up to forty pounds to some of those other
good horses, he can. But that's not the way I like it!"

"You're as sensitive to weight as an apothecary's scale," a
reporter in the back shouted.

"I better be," Henry answered gruffly through the screen
door. "No one else is or we wouldn't be assigned more
pounds than ever before in the Carter."

"Maybe he's more horse than ever raced in the Carter,"
someone suggested. "After all, Henry, it's the handicapper's
job to try to bring all horses down to the wire together."

"And it's my job and privilege to withdraw my entry from
a race when I think the weight assignment is excessive!"
Henry bellowed at the top of his voice.

The Black jumped and Alec had trouble quieting him.

The reporters too had jumped and were standing farther away from the door.

"What are you staying in here for?" Alec asked Henry. "You're getting him excited. He just might kick you."

"Hold him then," Henry said brusquely without leaving the stall.

A reporter asked quietly but with a sarcastic overtone, "Shall we tell our readers then that the Black's racing will be limited this season because of your aversion to high weights?"

"Tell 'em anything you want," Henry said, "but I say I won't start any horse when I think the weight assignment is unfair to him."

"Then the Black won't be meeting Casey this season?"

"That's up to the handicapper," Henry answered.

"And Eclipse?" another reporter asked. "What about him, Henry? Would you be interested in a special race Aqueduct would like to arrange between Eclipse, Casey and the Black?"

"That's still up to the handicapper," Henry said. "If he treats Eclipse like an ordinary three-year-old and has him too light-weighted against us I won't accept it. Some horses reach their peak at three years of age and Eclipse is one of 'em. He should not be weighted as a colt."

A reporter laughed and said kindly, "I agree with you, Henry, since he broke the Black's seven-furlong record last Saturday. But let's get back to the Carter. You're out of it and there'll be no Casey-Black race on Monday. Is that what you want us to tell our readers?"

"I told you to tell 'em anything you want," Henry shouted. The Black let go a hind leg against the wooden planking. It unnerved Henry and he jumped for the door.

The reporters laughed and Henry said furiously, "Get on with you now! All of you! Tell your readers that I'm not goin' to start a horse in a race when I think he has no chance to win! Now get out of here, I say!"

The Black snorted and half-reared, then his hind hoofs crashed the wood siding again. Henry left the stall, hurriedly chasing the newsmen from the barn.

When the trainer returned, Alec was kneeling in the straw feeling the Black's legs. He looked up and said, "I don't understand you, Henry. Here you are, more worried about his legs than you should be, and yet you come in here and cause a lot of excitement. We're lucky that he didn't hurt himself."

Henry said with concern, "I didn't figure on his kicking. He isn't lame, is he, Alec? I'd never forgive myself if he was. I really wouldn't. I mean it."

Alec shook his head. "No, I'm sure he's okay." Then he looked again at his friend whose voice a few minutes ago had been like the bellow of an angry bull. Now it was soft and kind, even a little sheepish. "Why'd you stay inside, Henry?"

"So they couldn't get a good look at my face through the screen. If I'd been outside, they'd have seen I was just kidding."

"You mean you're going to start the Black in the Carter?" Alec asked.

"Sure. Actually I didn't tell them I *wasn't* going to."

Alec shook his head in bewilderment. Then, trying to reconcile what he'd heard before with what he was now being told, he said, "I guess you're figuring he's certain to be second anyway and that's ten thousand dollars toward the barn. Is that it?"

"No, that isn't it," Henry answered quietly. "I'm figuring on pickin' up that first money of some forty-five thousand."

"Carrying one hundred and forty pounds against Casey?" Alec asked incredulously.

"Sure. The weight won't bother 'im at seven-eighths of a mile. He might have some trouble handling it over a mile but not at seven furlongs."

"Then why'd you make such a fuss?"

"You wouldn't want anyone to think I was *satisfied* with the weights, would you?" Henry asked impatiently. "Gosh, Alec, I'm surprised at you!"

Alec laughed as he straightened the Black's mane. "It's just that I've never heard you beef so much about weights before," he said. "You sound like a track lawyer. You really do."

"Sometimes you got to be one to get anywhere in this business," Henry answered. "Anyway it's goin' to be a hot weekend."

"With plenty of fireworks," Alec added, and Henry nodded in complete agreement.

The following Saturday began the long Fourth of July weekend. It was hot, as Henry had forecast, and Eclipse started off the fireworks. The burly brown horse came onto the track for the running of the Dwyer, which was exclusively for three-year-olds. There were just two others who went to the starting gate with him, and they were there only to pick up the tempting second and third purses.

"I wouldn't do it for any kind of money," Henry said, watching them. "It would be too humiliating for my colt. I couldn't stand it."

The fact that no one wanted to make a race of the classic

Dwyer Stakes was the final tribute to Eclipse's greatness. He stood alone in his age division and the crowd of more than forty thousand holiday fans knew that this would be his easiest triumph.

The big colt didn't let them down. While they watched a race that was no contest he won it in such a dramatic way that he proved himself once more to be a champion of champions.

Eclipse toyed with his two competitors until the home-stretch of the mile-and-a-quarter race. He had let them stay with him most of the way around and his enormous strides made it seem that he was simply loping along. The two other horses began tiring before the end of a mile but even then Eclipse's jockey did not take him to the front. Instead he let the big colt romp alongside while the others staggered wearily down the long homestretch.

Henry muttered angrily at what to him was an ignoble victory by Eclipse. "Those two will never be the same after this," he told Alec. "I've seen plenty of horses' hearts broken by doin' what he's doin' to them. Why doesn't Seymour take him on, anyway? What's he trying to prove, that he can win any time he pleases?"

Alec, too, was furious with the way Eclipse was being ridden. "Seymour's probably had orders not to let him go until he sees the white of the finish wire," he said sarcastically, "against two *outclassed* colts."

A quarter of a mile from the judges' stand Eclipse made his move. But Seymour did not bring him on immediately. Instead he dropped him behind the others and then took him to the middle of the track. There he let the big colt fly, and Eclipse came forward with the speed of a winged thunderbird in full and awesome flight.

Of all the thousands who were in the stands only Alec and Henry turned away. "If that's the only way I could make thirty-seven thousand bucks," Henry said, "I wouldn't have it."

Alec nodded and followed Henry down the aisle. "Well, we've got Monday's forty-five thousand dollars waiting for us in the barn. Let's go see him."

"Sure," Henry answered. "But I guess Casey's figuring on pickin' up that same money."

"Let's hope we get to it first."

"Of course," Henry said. "I wouldn't think of it any other way. One thing sure, it's not goin' to be a race like we saw today."

Boom!

16

Monday was hotter and more humid than Saturday had been but more than thirty-five thousand persons filled Aqueduct's stands. They had come to see their own special kind of Fourth of July fireworks, the explosive clash between Casey and the Black in the Carter Handicap.

Alec went from the stable area to the jockeys' room, tiny wisps of dust rising from beneath the soles of his leather moccasins as he walked. Despite the water sprinklers the track, too, would be dry—very sandy and very dry. This racing strip had to be a little wet to be fast. Rain would have helped it and made life a lot more comfortable for everybody.

Alec felt the sweat drip down the back of his neck and decided that if he hurried he'd just have time enough for a shower. He went through the crowded jockeys' room and sat down on the bench in front of his locker. He talked to the men around him while he undressed and then he went into the showers. When he came out again a number of the jockeys had left to ride in the fourth race. Those who remained were reading or playing cards or just sitting. Alec passed Billy Watts, who was studying his red-and-green silks as if he'd never seen them before.

Alec hesitated and then stopped. "Hi, Billy," he said. He waited, drying himself all over again with his big towel. One never knew quite what to do when a jockey felt as Billy did. It was so easy to say the wrong thing or look the wrong way.

"Hello, Alec." Billy Watts glanced at Alec and then turned back to his locker. He seemed embarrassed as he quickly withdrew his white nylon pants and started getting into them. The back pocket had a small rip and he fingered it nervously while waiting for Alec to leave.

"You ought to get your girl to mend that for you," Alec said lightly.

"After today I won't be using them," Billy said in sudden defiance. "No more worrying about making weights and following riding orders. No more of that stuff for me."

Alec went on to his own locker. *No more fear of crowding and slamming with steel-shod hoofs all around you,* he thought. *No more fear of violent death. Feeling as you do, you're well out of it, Billy. After today you can just worry about mares and colts.*

He had finished dressing when the riders came back from the fourth race and a few departed for the fifth. Some stripped off their wet silks and headed for the showers, through for the day. But the great majority hung around, resting and rerunning the fourth race, even accusing each other angrily of interference and dangerous riding.

Alec listened but said nothing even though once in a while they asked him for his opinion on a hot point at issue. There was a day not so long ago, he recalled, when instead of turning to him as an experienced rider and arbitrator they'd made him the brunt of their violent verbal attacks.

Their accusations of one another were all part of the game. There had been no fouls committed in the fourth race. There would be no hideous revenge, as was being threatened, the next time out. They all talked a fiercer game than they played, for they knew that every stride of each race was being photographed by the film patrol. If there was a foul the cameras would show it and the guilty jockey would hear of it very, very soon afterward from the judges. But it always helped to be explosive between races even though it was a shock to the nervous system of the inexperienced rider. However, Alec reminded himself, it wouldn't be long before he, too, would speak angry and bitter words in turn.

A tall boy, too tall and heavy to be a jockey much longer, came over and sat down beside Alec.

"Who'd Henry think he was kiddin', anyway?" he asked.

From the caked dust on the boy's face Alec could tell he'd been pretty far back in the previous race. "What do you mean, Skip?" he asked.

"This business of not startin' the Black in the Carter. Everybody knew he was goin' to drop his name in the entry box yesterday. Everybody did, so why'd he do it?"

Alec smiled. "Why does Henry do anything? I don't know. You'd better ask him."

"Not me. I wouldn't get near that guy with a fifty-foot pole. I wouldn't even ride for him. Not even if he gave me the horse. That's how much I wouldn't get near him. He scares me. I mean it!"

Alec stood up and shoved his goggles in his back pocket. Another boy joined them. He was much smaller than Alec and bowlegged. When he carried a saddle, the girth and stirrups dragged on the ground unless he put the whole thing on top of his head.

"Yeah," the little jockey remarked, "I agree with what Skip says about Henry always tryin' to be a wise guy. And there's something else he does that ain't very smart, either."

Alec smiled at the sound of the boy's high, droll voice that went so well with the rest of him. "What is it, Chub?" he asked. Tiny rivulets of sweat were running down the jockey's dust-caked face. It was evident that he hadn't been out in front any more than Skip in the fourth race.

"I mean this business of everybody thinkin' of the Carter as a special race just between Casey an' the Black. What do they think the rest of us will be doin' anyway? That's what I'd like to know. What do they think anyway? Huh?"

Alec shook his head. "I don't know," he answered quietly. "But I can't see that's Henry's fault. It's a horse race."

It was time to go. Most of the jockeys had already left the room. Michael Costello tossed the magazine he'd been reading to one side and glanced Alec's way. He didn't say anything to him before leaving. His black eyes were somber.

"Let's go," Alec told the boys.

"Yeah," Skip said. "Why not?"

"Sure." Chub smiled. "Like Alec says, it's a horse race."

The jockeys' room, now almost empty, was quiet except for the drip of the showers. Sixteen men, not boys any longer, had gone to mount sixteen horses for a winner's purse of forty-five thousand dollars. To them it was more than a special race between two famous stars. Handicap horses didn't scare easily, and neither did their riders.

Something can always happen to the big shots in a big field like this, they figured. *Didn't some wise guy once count a hundred and fifty ways in which a horse can lose a race? So how're you going to protect Casey and the Black against odds like that? Give us an inch and we'll take a mile. Give us a chance at a buck and we'll take forty-five. Thousand, that is. Our cut is ten percent, that's four thousand five hundred take-home pay. Come on, Jock, get off those scales and get movin'. We got a horse race on our hands.*

The Clerk of the Scales said, "Ramsay. Number thirteen. One hundred and forty. Check. Next.

"Watts. Number seven. One hundred and twenty. Check.

"Costello. Number three. One hundred and thirty-five. Check. Hurry it up, fellas. We're late now.

"Smith. Number sixteen. One hundred even. Check."

Alec had his number 13 high on his arm when he saw Billy Watts looking at it. He didn't like what he saw in Billy's eyes so he said quickly, "Think of all the malteds you'll be drinking after this one. No more scales. Lucky guy."

The young jockey didn't answer and Alec left for the paddock where Henry and the Black were awaiting him.

Beneath the green-and-white striped roof he saw his horse in the number 13 stall and the crowd that stood nearby. Pushing his way through, he went to the Black. The stallion stopped pawing when Alec ran a hand over his shoulder blades, rubbing him gently. The Black was wet but not too wet, considering the kind of day it was and all the people milling around. There probably wasn't a dry horse in the shed, including Casey.

Henry said, "He's down to bedrock. A little jittery but full of run. The crowd gave 'im a hand when I brought 'im around the track. He was all set to go then. If it hadn't been for Napoleon—"

Alec rubbed the Black's muzzle and felt the breath hot on his hand. "He likes the crowd. I really think he's starting to play up to it," Alec said.

"I hope not," Henry growled. "The filly cured me of all that. I jus' want 'im to run like he can, crowd or no crowd."

The call to the post came and Henry boosted Alec into the saddle.

"Any orders?" Alec asked.

"Just go about your business," Henry said simply. Mounting Napoleon, he kept close beside the Black while the first few horses filed from the paddock and went up the dirt ramp leading to the track.

Billy Watts rode by, his face unusually white and set.

"What's the matter with him?" Henry asked.

"I offered him a job at the farm and he took it," Alec answered quietly.

"Oh," Henry said and nothing more. It wasn't necessary. There was only one reason for a jockey to quit when he could still make the weights and get mounts.

Mike Costello rode by on Casey and the Black snorted as if he knew that there was the horse to beat. Mike raised his whip and waved to them.

Henry nodded back but he told Alec, "Don't go expecting any favors from him like y'did the last time. He might love you like a father but he won't give you an inch of track."

"He won't need to," Alec said. "This race is between horses, not jockeys."

"Yeah," Henry agreed, "they'll do the running, all right. To hear some people talk you wouldn't know it, though. To them the race is strictly a contest between you and Mike."

"And fourteen other jocks," Alec added, smiling.

Henry grunted as the Black swerved hard against Napoleon, almost toppling the gray gelding.

"That was a close one," the trainer said, regaining his balance with his mount. They pressed their combined weights against the Black while Alec rubbed his horse's shoulder blades, quieting him.

It was their turn to go.

"All seven furlongs calls for is speed," Henry said, leading the Black up the ramp. "He set the record last time out. Eclipse broke it. Now go out and break it again."

Alec took a snug hold on the reins as they stepped onto the track. From the clubhouse and the stands to their left came a thunderous ovation. The post parade had begun. People spilled out from beneath the stands where they'd gone to escape the hot sun and rushed to the rails.

"Are you still crying about the weights, Henry?" someone shouted to the trainer. "Whatya think about giving the *great* Casey five whole pounds?"

Henry called back, "They should be reversed. Casey oughta be givin' us five pounds!"

Alec loosened his hold slightly and the Black stepped ahead of Napoleon. But the stallion didn't pull away and Alec had no trouble keeping him to a walk while the long line of sixteen horses passed the stands. They turned around at the middle of the homestretch and came down again. This time they rounded the first turn at a lope and went toward the chute adjoining the backstretch where the race would begin.

Alec didn't watch the others. There were too many of them, both riders and horses. There was no strategy to be planned and executed in such a large field at so short a distance. As Henry had said, seven-eighths of a mile was no more than a long sprint, calling for sheer speed and little courage and stamina. Yet the purse was high. There were few richer sprints. That's why there was a field of this size. *Anything could happen* in such a race and the money was not going begging.

Henry had told him to go about his business, Alec recalled, and that's all he could do. Get out in front as soon as possible and stay there. No holding back today. Nothing but speed.

Alec continued rubbing the Black to quiet him. Henry kept them on the far outside of the banked turn, not wanting to look for trouble. Far up the line Casey was cantering.

"The great Casey," the man back on the rail had called him, and he was surely a good-looking horse today. His coat was as wet as the Black's and shone golden in the sun, while his muscles slid gracefully beneath tightly drawn skin. He was turned out beautifully and there was no doubt that he was fit. He'd won five big races so far this season, all of them under high weight, and all in record time. Actually, Casey seemed to be getting stronger as the season's campaign wore on. This was the first race in which he wasn't carrying top weight.

Alec turned away from Casey and looked across at Aqueduct's infield, which had the greenest grass he'd ever seen. Unlike Belmont Park there was nothing planted here to obstruct the crowd's view of the racing strip itself. Only a small lake and a few low and well-kept hedges dotted the grassy plot. The far stands were painted green. All in all everything looked cool, affording some relief on this very hot day.

The horses turned up the chute at the head of the backstretch and went to the seven-furlong pole where the starting gate awaited them. As Henry and Alec went behind it Henry said, "Well, here's where I get off." He glanced at

Alec and then at the number 13 on his arm. "It's a good thing we're not superstitious," he added.

"Jet Pilot won the Kentucky Derby from the thirteenth box," Alec reminded him.

"Your memory is better than mine," Henry said. "Luck to you, Alec." He stayed there as if reluctant to leave until an assistant starter waved him off. It was the longest time Alec had known Henry to remain behind the gate and he wondered about it.

Most of the other horses were already in their stalls, and now one of the starter's crew was running toward the Black. Everything was being done in a hurry even though the official starter, high on his platform just off the track, had called, "Take it easy now, all of you. No hurry now. No hurry at all."

Who was he trying to kid? Alec wondered.

Alec waved the crewman back when the Black struck out in his mounting excitement. "I'll take him in," he called. "Go ahead." His voice sounded as shrill as everybody else's.

"Okay," the crewman yelled back, reaching for the next horse's bridle instead of the Black's.

The assistant starters had the front and back cage doors of all the stalls shut with the exception of the last four. Then stalls 14, 15 and 16 were closed, leaving only the Black outside the gate.

"Ramsay," the official starter called through his amplifier, "get your horse in but don't rush him. We don't want any trouble. We got plenty of time. Just watch him. Be careful. I know *him*."

Alec was well aware that at the slightest touch of a button the starter could cut the electric current from the magnets holding the doors shut. It would happen the very second he got the Black inside his stall. The starter wouldn't wait.

"Easy, fellow, easy," Alec said softly, taking his horse forward. He wondered if it was his heart or the Black's that was making all the noise. He had his horse's forequarters inside the stall.

Alec caught a glimpse of Billy Watts's face in the number 7 stall as Gunfire rose high and then came down hard against the padded sides.

"No chance! No chance, sir!" Billy shouted at the top of his lungs.

Suddenly almost all the jockeys were yelling. Only Michael Costello was quiet, sitting on his tall, slick-muscled Casey. Far across the infield the crowd impatiently awaited the start of the Carter Handicap. Alec moved the Black all the way into his stall.

Then the big bell rang and the doors flew open! Sixteen horses burst from their boxes and overflowed the track, their glistening bodies jamming against one another while their riders screamed for racing room!

The Black broke from the wrong lead and took his first stride in the air as Alec brought him down. When he was straightened out again and running, Alec saw that the inside horses were in the shape of a flying wedge with the light-weighted number 6 horse in the lead and trying to "steal" the race from the very beginning. The horse had a good two lengths' start on those nearest to him and was increasing it with the sure, swift strides of a top sprinter. Only ninety-five pounds were on his back, and Alec wondered if the Black, carrying forty-five pounds more, could possibly catch him after so poor a start.

On the far outside of the track was another horse who had broken fast and now was being eased across the Black's path toward the flying wedge with its fast-sprinting leader. Alec noted that it was the number 16 horse, ridden by Smith and carrying just one hundred pounds.

Alec made no attempt to move any closer to the rail. He didn't want to save ground. All he wanted for the Black was plenty of racing room, and he had it there in the middle of the track with most of the backstretch still before them. It was a long run to the far turn, longer than at Belmont or any other track in the New York area, for Aqueduct's turns were short and sharp.

He waited patiently for the Black to settle into full racing stride but his eyes were anxious while he watched the jamming, yelling pack to his left. All fury had broken loose there and only the Black and the two light-weighted pace setters were clear of it. Where was Casey anyway?

Glancing back, Alec saw that Casey was caught in the back of the wedge with Mike Costello trying desperately to take him out of it. Alec clucked to his horse. By the time Casey got clear of that traffic jam he'd have the Black well up with the front runners and neither Casey nor any other horse was going to catch him from behind.

The Black's strides were coming longer and faster, and the sprinting light-weights ahead stopped pulling away. Soon they'd be dropping back to him, very soon now. Alec knew he'd have them by the time they swept into the sharp, high-banked turn. The Black must have known it too, for his ears suddenly pitched forward and stayed there while the ground gave way between him and the leaders. He was moving into full flight and going up!

"Here we come!" shouted Alec. He brought his left hand down upon the Black's extended neck, easing him across the track. They were about to fly into the sharp turn and he didn't want their speed to carry them to the outer rim. As he reached the crown of the track he noticed that the two front-running leaders were going a bit wide as they swung into the sharp turn. The opening they'd left on the rail was very small but for a fleeting second Alec considered taking the Black through it.

There was a horse racing just to his left and Alec decided against making for the hole. It was too risky and he was in a good enough position now to pass the leaders when they came off the turn into the homestretch. The Black should win this race with ease, he thought, for unlike Casey they'd run into no trouble, *thanks to their outside post position.*

He sat still on his horse, taking up rein while rounding the turn. Behind him he could hear the pounding of the jammed field and the wordless yelling of the jockeys. He was very happy to be in front and well out of such a melee.

To his left raced the horse which had managed to escape the wedge as they'd gone into the turn. Alec glanced at him for the first time and saw that it was *Gunfire!* He couldn't see Billy Watts's face, for the boy was riding low on the opposite side and whipping his mount!

Alec wondered why Billy hadn't waited for the long stretch run before making his bid for the lead. Then he saw Gunfire's head pointed for the slight opening on the rail and knew that Billy had decided to try to slip through!

Out of the corner of his eye Alec watched Gunfire charge for the hole. If Billy was successful in squeezing him through, he'd be the one to beat. If not, he'd be in a bucketful of trouble with no place to go.

Billy Watts had no time to stop Gunfire's move when the leaders, coming off the sharp turn, suddenly swept back to the rail. No longer was there an opening! Billy snatched at the reins and stood in his stirrups, his face deathly white. For a second there was danger that Gunfire would go down but he managed to stay erect and keep going.

Racing alongside, Alec saw Billy's saddle suddenly slip from beneath him! He realized that the leathers had broken under the strain of slowing the gelding. Now Gunfire was in full racing stride again and Billy was half off, his feet tangled in the loose stirrup irons! To their rear pounded the tons of steel-shod hoofs that Billy Watts had been going to leave behind forever after today.

Alec pulled the Black over to the free-running gelding and grabbed Billy's shoulders, holding him until the jockey had righted himself. Even then he couldn't take away his support, for the saddle had slipped underneath Gunfire and the stirrups were dangling dangerously close to his legs. If they tripped him, he'd go down and Billy's only chance of escape would be to hang on to Alec—if the Black didn't go down too.

Stride for stride raced the two horses, the Black snorting in frustration at the tight grip on his mouth and the long stretch run still before him. Alec managed to hold Billy on Gunfire and still keep his own seat. Suddenly they were surrounded on all sides by the jam-packed field! For a flashing second Alec thought he saw Mike Costello riding alongside, keeping the others away from them. If there was any bumping now, the Black would go down too. Alec wasn't sure it was Mike who was running interference for them. He was too busy trying to keep his balance and Billy's.

Nor did Alec hear the tremendous roar from the stands when the danger of being bumped was over. The applause was for Casey as he unleashed his explosive "kick" during the last quarter of a mile and worked his way through the pack like a broken field runner in full touchdown flight.

Later, newsmen likened Casey's victory charge to the boom of a Fourth of July cannon whose firing would be heard around the racing world. Their unbelieving eyes and the click of their stopwatches told them so.

Alec heard only the click of eternity, which wasn't difficult to do when a rider leans from one horse to another at racing speed. At the moment he didn't care who won the race. He was lucky to be getting back in one piece, and so was Billy Watts.

Bust

17

That evening the jockeys had a party and Alec Ramsay was the guest of honor. They gave him a handsome gold wrist watch for preventing an accident which easily could have been fatal.

Later Alec joined Henry back at Belmont Park. He found the trainer sitting alone on the porch steps. It was late and the only noise to be heard was the occasional nicker of a stabled horse.

"How'd it go?" the trainer asked.

Alec raised his hand so Henry could see the luminous dial. "It was nice of them," he said.

Henry grunted. "The watch is nothing," he said. "They meant a lot more than that."

"Any one of them would have done the same thing," Alec said.

"I hope so. I'm not so old that I've forgotten what all of you got in common out there. You've got to stick together while you're tryin' to beat each other."

Alec sat down beside Henry. "One thing certain," he said, "is that you can't walk out on somebody in trouble. Not for any kind of money."

"Forget the purse," Henry said. "I told you we'd make it up."

"We have a long way to go to a hundred thousand."

"Not so long if he stays sound." ·

"He cooled off all right," Alec said. "There's nothing wrong with him."

"The left foreleg," Henry said with concern. "I'm worried. He skipped again goin' into his stall."

"He plays," Alec answered. "Sometimes during a race he'll strike out and scarcely break stride."

"I hope you're right."

"I'm right, all right."

"Anyway, if the handicapper just leaves him alone now," Henry said. "If he just don't put any more weight on him."

"After today's race Casey will be the one who gets top weight," Alec said.

"Sure," Henry agreed. "At the end he was just playin' with the others. I never saw such a finish as he put on."

Alec glanced at his watch. "They should have given this to Mike for keeping the pack clear of us."

Henry nodded. "He sure acted as a blocking back for you. But don't go givin' him your watch. That's all you got out of the race. He got forty-five thousand dollars."

"His stable did, you mean."

"Well, four thousand five hundred for Mike, then. That still beats a gold watch."

"You said yourself it was more than a watch." Alec smiled.

"Sure. And I meant it. So did they, even old Mike."

"What's next?" Alec asked, wanting to change the subject.

"The Brooklyn Handicap on Saturday," Henry said. "We can't let any fifty-thousand-dollar races go beggin'."

"Casey again?"

"Of course," Henry answered. "It's the big one for him. He's won the Metropolitan and the Suburban so only the Brooklyn is missing to complete the 'Triple.' Only two horses in well over fifty years have won all three races, and I suspect Casey'll be sent out to make it three for three and go down in racing history. That's the way I figure it, anyway."

"The handicap horse's Triple Crown," Alec mused.

"That's what it is, all right. Most horses who have won the Metropolitan Mile get beaten when the distance goes up to a mile and a quarter in the Suburban and the Brooklyn."

"It seems Casey can go up or down," Alec said. "He can sprint with the sprinters and stay with the stayers."

"So can we," Henry said emphatically. "The Black was sprinting before Billy Watts fouled us up."

Alec lapsed into silence a moment and then said thoughtfully, "Billy was trying to prove something."

"To whom, the stands?" Henry asked. "He knew darn well that opening on the rail was too small to use."

"No, it wasn't," Alec corrected. "He could have squeezed through if it hadn't closed on him. But I imagine it looked pretty small to him at that."

"What do you mean?"

"Feeling the way Billy did, a 'hole' can look even smaller than it is."

"Oh," Henry said. "You mean he was tryin' to prove something to himself?"

Alec nodded. "And he did, I believe. He didn't go around the horses as he might have done."

Henry said thoughtfully, "I guess so, Alec. I guess you're right at that. Now Billy can quit, knowin' he's licked what bothered him. When's he going to the farm?"

"Tomorrow morning," Alec answered.

"Good," Henry said. "We can use him up there."

"Guess we'd better quit ourselves," Alec said, getting to his feet.

Henry rose too. "I hope you mean just for the night." He put an arm around the boy's shoulders as they went up the steps.

"Sure." Alec smiled. "Just for the night. I'm tired. It's been a long day."

"And not an easy one," Henry agreed soberly, his arm still around the boy. "But you made it all the way around and considering everything—" His voice lingered in the still night air while he and Alec Ramsay went inside.

We'll get them in the Brooklyn, Alec. That race will separate the men from the boys, all right. Mark my words, Casey will know he's been in a ding-dong of a fight.

But the next morning Henry decided there'd be no Brooklyn Handicap for the Black. It took him one second to change his mind, just long enough to read the published weights for the horses entered in the big race. He looked at the 146 pounds opposite the Black's name, mumbled something violently to himself, and then said clearly to Alec, "He's out!"

Alec didn't ask any questions. He just looked at Henry's face, which had flushed deep red in anger. He waited a long while before Henry's face was its normal color again. Even then he waited for the trainer to break the fierce silence.

Finally Henry shook his head vigorously. "I can't believe it, Alec. I just can't believe it, much less try to understand it. No track handicapper in the world—" His words came faster, tumbling over each other in still another incoherent burst of anger.

Alec managed to get the list from Henry's hand. He noted the 146 pounds assigned to the Black and just below it the 136 pounds for Casey. Only then did he understand completely the fury that possessed Henry, for it filled him too.

"I've always supported and been proud of New York racing but I'm through now, Alec," Henry shouted. "I tell you I'm through!"

"It's a lot of weight, all right," Alec agreed with feeling.

"A lot of weight?" Henry repeated as if aghast at the mildness of Alec's words. "Why, I've never heard of any horse carryin' that much weight in the Brooklyn or any other race of this kind!"

"He's got Casey down at one hundred and thirty-six," Alec said, nodding his head soberly.

"Are we supposed to feel *flattered* because the Black gets ten pounds more than the horse that walloped him yesterday?" Henry asked incredulously. "Is that it?"

Alec attempted to calm Henry down. "We sure must have impressed somebody in those first few furlongs," he said with feigned lightness. "I'm afraid it was the track handicapper."

"That's all he's goin' to see of us!" Henry bellowed, tearing up the weight sheets. "We're movin' out of here, Alec. We're goin' where we won't be humiliated any longer. I'd be crazy to start him again in New York."

Alec waited a few minutes and then said, "It's going to

cost money to move, Henry, and we don't have much left. Maybe he can carry the weight. It's only six pounds more than he had yesterday."

"Alec!" Henry shouted. "Only six pounds more but over a mile and a quarter route. He couldn't handle it and still spot Casey ten pounds! It would be disgraceful and humiliating to ask him to try."

Alec studied Henry's set face. This was no tirade put on to impress anyone. Henry was deadly serious. Alec had no doubt that he wouldn't start the Black in the Brooklyn Handicap under such a weight assignment.

Henry said more quietly, "Look at it this way, Alec. Using most handicappers' rule-of-thumb methods in translatin' pounds to lengths at a mile and a quarter, we'd be spottin' Casey *five* lengths by giving 'im ten pounds."

"You mean it figures that two pounds represents a length of a horse at the finish wire over that distance?" Alec asked.

Henry nodded. "And we're not givin' the great Casey that kind of a handicap here or any place else. When we find a handicapper that treats us fair and square we'll race the Black again but not before!"

The press were waiting at the barn for Henry. He told them just what he'd told Alec. And like Alec they believed him this time. They knew Henry's moods and this was one with which they could not fool or change.

A noted sports columnist said finally, "That knocks the wind right out of our buildup for Saturday's 'Race of the Century.'"

"You've still got Casey," Henry replied brusquely. "He wants the Brooklyn so bad he'll probably go to the post even at the top weight he's been assigned. Only two others have carried a hundred and thirty-six in the whole history of the race. You might tell your readers that," he added sarcastically.

"Oh, we've got Eclipse too," the columnist said. "We just came from his barn."

"You got what . . . ?" Henry asked incredulously.

"Eclipse," the columnist repeated. "He's going in the Brooklyn at a hundred and sixteen pounds. Haven't you read the complete list yet?"

Henry took the paper handed to him. Far down the list of fifty-five horses who'd been nominated May 15 for the Brooklyn Handicap was Eclipse. And he was assigned only 116 pounds!

"Now I *know* everybody's crazy," Henry said.

A few of the reporters laughed but most of them remained solemnly quiet. One of the latter said, "He's stepping out of his age division again, Henry, and over a route this time, not a sprint like before. I guess he's serious about meeting the Black and Casey."

"He won't get to meet the Black ever," Henry said emphatically. "Not carryin' such a ridiculous weight assignment."

A young reporter said, almost too courteously to be friendly, "Mr. Dailey, I'm rather new in racing but as I understand it there's a traditional weight-for-age scale, made by the Jockey Club, which most track handicappers use in arriving at their weight assignments for a race. Is that correct?"

"You'd have to ask a handicapper," Henry replied curtly. "But I imagine he'd start off from the scale anyway."

"Well then," the reporter went on, "you claim that Eclipse's one-hundred-and-sixteen-pound assignment is ridiculous. Yet according to the official scale that's exactly what a three-year-old should carry at a mile and a quarter during the month of July when racing older horses."

Henry grimaced. "It's still ridiculous," he said patiently. "I've said it before and I'll say it again. Eclipse is no ordinary three-year-old and should not be weighted as such. You don't have to listen to me. *Look at the record, three new track marks in his last three times out!* Assigning Eclipse weight according to the traditional scale is unfair to those racin' against 'im! I won't have any part of it!"

The young reporter smiled. He had Henry Dailey going, and it would make good copy. He didn't stop to wonder why all the others in the group were very still and solemn.

"Unfair, you say?" he prodded Henry. "Don't you think it more unfair to ask a young horse to race an older one at equal weights?"

"I didn't say equal weights," Henry retorted, losing his patience with the man. "I said *fair* weights. Eclipse is going much too light and the Black much too heavy."

"Oh, then the Black *is* going in the Brooklyn?" the reporter asked naively.

"No, he *isn't!*" Henry exploded.

"Tell me," the young man went on hurriedly, not wanting to lose his newly won advantage over the trainer, "don't you think, too, that it's unfair to ask a young horse to knock himself out, probably even break his heart, racing against two older stars like the Black and Casey?"

Henry could feel the blood rushing to his face and he shook his head angrily. He caught his lower lip between his teeth and waited a moment before answering. When he spoke his voice was trembling but coherent.

"You mean like Eclipse broke the heart of those two

horses *his own age* in the Dwyer a couple of Saturdays ago? Is that what you mean? Do you think they'll ever race again? Do you?"

The young reporter didn't answer and those about him began moving for the barn door.

"Well, sir," Henry went on, visibly trying to control himself, "I've always believed that no horse will be hurt in any way, regardless of what you ask of him, *providin'* he's in the proper physical shape to do it. Eclipse is that kind of a horse. He's big and at his peak. He could meet older horses every day of the week and never feel it. The only heart-breaking to consider is that which he's done himself."

The newsmen wrote their stories. Most of them agreed with Henry, and it turned out that their readers did likewise. Horsemen, too, nodded their heads in agreement with Henry's view of the weight assignments for the Brooklyn Handicap. It was definitely stated that very few trainers would send their handicap horses against the lightly weighted Eclipse. It was rumored that the great Casey's name too would be missing from the entry box Friday morning. Michael Costello was especially bitter, for he felt that at level weights no horse in the world was so fast as his Casey, but that giving twenty pounds to Eclipse was too much. "The very divil himself has a-taken over the Old One in the office," he protested vigorously. " 'Tis honest weights we want."

The track handicapper remained silent and adamant despite all criticism. He issued just one brief public statement to the effect that it was his job to give every horse in a race a fair chance at first money. He had enjoyed his work for some forty years now and would continue to perform his duties to the best of his ability until replaced. There would be no changes in his weight assignments for the Brooklyn Handicap.

After reading the handicapper's statement Henry told Alec, "Well, that's that. We're not racin' Saturday."

But Henry didn't reckon with the track president. Thursday morning the value of the Brooklyn Handicap was raised to $100,000 plus the nomination and entrance money. It meant, according to the front office's release to the newspapers, that for the first time in the history of the Brooklyn Handicap the winner would be assured of $100,000.

The final portion of the statement read, "It is the management's hope that in making this year's Brooklyn Handicap one of the richest races in the country we will bring about the greatest race of modern times. We sincerely hope that those trainers who have disappointed racing enthusiasts the world over by their public announcements not to race in the Brooklyn Handicap will now reconsider in light of the larger purse."

That very day Casey's trainer announced to the press that his chestnut champion would surely start on Saturday. "I don't like the twenty-pound difference between my horse and Eclipse any more now than I did before," he said. "But for a hundred thousand dollars we'd take a crack at Pegasus himself."

Later that evening Henry Dailey said, "The track management has touched us where it hurts. Everybody knows we could use a hundred thousand dollars for a new barn. We aim to try and get it in one fell swoop on Saturday. Furthermore, I'd like to say this. I'm glad the front office statement didn't cite 'sportsmanship and the best interests of racing' in order to get these three big horses together. I honestly don't feel it's fair or good sportsmanship to send us off at such great difference in weights. I'm afraid Saturday will bear me out but I'm hopin' for some kind of a break in a large field that will offset the weight differences."

Three in a Row

18

"The Old One in the office," as Michael Costello had referred to the track handicapper, was truly old. His hair, what there was of it, was snow white and his hands shook involuntarily when he carefully figured out his weight assignments. But he wore no glasses and believed his eyes to be as keen as ever. They'd helped make his weighted ratings of horses one of the best guides of true champions or those on their way to the top. Usually when he packed a high impost upon a horse his judgment proved to be sound. Usually but not always.

The Old One hadn't liked the way Casey had won the Carter Handicap the preceding Monday. At 135 pounds the chestnut horse had cut down the others in the stretch as if they'd been just play for him. It must never happen again. Not that he sympathized with the underdog. No, it was simply that there never should be a *badly beaten* underdog. He had failed utterly to give every horse a chance at first money.

Was he perhaps getting too old, as a few of the newspapers had intimated? Were his eyes as keen as he believed them to be?

That week he watched the final workouts of the three big stars very closely, paying more attention to them than he'd ever done to any horses in his life. He must be certain he was right this time. He'd taken too much criticism and abuse from friends and press alike. Of course he could not change the weights he had assigned for the Brooklyn Handicap but it would do no harm to verify his judgment.

As he watched Casey come onto the Aqueduct track his eyes were very sharp and unwavering but he trembled as if with chill. Usually he didn't reach the track quite so early in the morning. He found it a little more difficult getting up these days and it took him a little longer to get going. Also, he drove to the track a little slower, a little more carefully. But he never missed much once he got there.

A good handicapper must take into consideration the physical condition of his horses.

He studied the glowing son of Bold Irishman. Yes, Casey was in the full bloom of health despite all his hot-weather racing. He was eager too. He fairly jumped into his workout.

The Old One's thumb pressed the stem of his big and ancient stopwatch.

A good handicapper must keep an accurate work sheet of his horses.

"Twenty-four and three . . . fifty seconds even . . . one thirteen and four . . . finishing off the mile in one forty flat. Slow enough for him."

Casey had seemed to relish his work. He'd wanted to go more that last quarter but Costello had snugged him close. He came back prancing and not breathing hard at all. An early-morning crowd followed him to the barn.

The Old One nodded his uncovered white head. Yes, he was right about Casey. At least he was pretty sure he was right. Oh, he could have put a little more weight on him than he had. But if he'd done so, he would have had to raise the Black even higher. That would've been too much to ask of any horse. The wisest solution was what he'd done, drop Eclipse to 116 pounds. That would bring Eclipse and Casey down to the wire together—at least, the way he figured it.

His gaze shifted to the thick-bodied colt coming through the track gate. Eclipse was ready to go at anything, at any time. He'd put on flesh, hot-weather racing or not. He'd developed such a chest they'd had to get a longer girth to go around him before he could be saddled for the Dwyer. A good handicapper needed to know such things.

Eclipse was being turned around in the middle of the track. He stood still a moment, looking a little lazy and lopsided. Then Robinson, his jockey, touched him lightly with his whip and he was off.

It was said that Eclipse needed company to work and race his best but the Old One knew it to be idle talk. Alone the big colt just looked sluggish because there was no horse with which to compare his way of going and the length of his strides. Now if one had a stopwatch and kept track of the quarters while Eclipse reeled them off—

"Twenty-two and one . . . forty-five even . . ."

The Old One's eyes left his watch and widened incredulously as they followed the colt. This was a very sharp work. This was an exhibition of speed one expected to see only in the afternoon, the very best afternoon on the very best track. His eyes narrowed as he glanced again at his watch.

"One o nine and two for three-quarters—" That was a second faster than the track mark and Robinson had a hold on him!

Another quarter slipped by with Eclipse being eased off but still flying. The crowd of trainers and boys near the rail were cheering him on but neither the colt nor Robinson seemed to be listening.

"One thirty-three and three," the Old One said aloud, snapping his watch at the end of a mile. "They didn't go faster than that, not until *he* came along."

The Old One followed Eclipse to the barn. He stood there with many others, watching the sweated colt being rubbed and scrubbed. His keen eyes never left the horse, not even when the three-year-old champion was being walked in a bright red cooler and only his head and hoofs were on display.

Finally, the Old One turned away. For all Eclipse's brilliance, he decided, the colt was not Casey's equal. He must believe in himself and especially his figures of the week before when he'd worked everything out for the Brooklyn Handicap. At a mile and a quarter, carrying equal weights, Casey was ten lengths the better horse. So Casey must carry twenty pounds more than Eclipse to bring them to the wire together.

The Old One held his lower lip still by biting on it. *Fantastic?* That's what everybody seemed to think of his weight assignment for Eclipse, and there were moments, moments like this when he— No, he mustn't even think it! If he had no faith in himself, what had he left?

Eagerly he returned to the track and his eyes found the Black. *Now, there was a horse.* There was one to remember and never, never forget. He rushed to the rail and stood still, his watch in his hand, his eyes on the tall black stallion who was being galloped the wrong way of the track.

Henry Dailey, riding Napoleon, was restraining him but he seemed most anxious to perform his chores. They came to a stop at the eighth pole and the Black was turned to face the infield.

"Ah," the Old One sighed to himself. It came out as it might if one were looking upon the work of a master.

There was no doubt that Henry Dailey had this horse ready to race, and when the Black was ready—well, remember Chicago? Or had everybody forgotten? Not that it was so long ago, but many other fast horses had come and gone since then. In this business one was inclined to see only what was directly before him. That is, if he was not a track handicapper whose business it was to remember as well as to record.

The Black spun quickly, his long strides coming so fast that he was in full run when he passed under the finish wire for the once-around-the-track trip. Alec Ramsay was riding very low and close so it was difficult for anyone to see how much he was asking of his mount. Afterward many people claimed he'd sat perfectly still all the way around. Others said he'd waved his hand alongside the Black's head, urging him on—and had gotten no response.

The Old One said nothing. He returned to his office and placed the watch on his huge desk. He looked at the face of it for a long, long time.

The Black had worked a very slow mile although he'd seemed to be going all-out. But Alec Ramsay could do more with the flick of his fingers and the pressure of his legs than any other jockey in the business. For all anyone knew the Black could have been under a very tight hold even though there was no indication of it. It was seldom, if ever, that one saw more coordination between horse and rider than was the case with Alec and the Black.

The Old One continued to look at his watch. The figures were :24.3, :51, 1:14.3, and the mile in 1:42, two seconds slower than even Casey's time. And unlike Casey the Black had been scheduled for a fast work, according to Henry Dailey's statement to the newspapers the night before.

The Old One got to his feet and nervously paced the room. Was he so completely wrong in his estimate of the Black's speed? Was the great horse *actually* five lengths faster than Casey, fifteen lengths faster than Eclipse at even weights, as he believed? Or was he instead being carried away by the memory of a race in Chicago years ago? Was he a sentimental old fool in believing the Black was fit and ready to equal that performance? Saturday would tell.

Three in a row they stepped onto the track following the call to the post for the Brooklyn Handicap. Number 1, Eclipse . . . number 2, Casey . . . number 3, the Black. There were no other entries.

Never before in the long history of the famous handicap had so many other eligibles for the race been so lightly weighted, but their trainers decided to leave this "Race of the Century" strictly alone. They didn't even send a horse out to walk around the track, if nothing else, to collect fourth-place money. Instead they sent a little note to the track management: "—two thousand five hundred dollars, courtesy of the trainers who will sit this one out and watch."

Henry on Napoleon said, "Not even a couple more horses to maybe cause Eclipse and Casey a stumble or two. No breaks today. Nothin' but trouble."

Alec didn't answer. He talked only to the Black, not in

words or sounds but merely by soft and gentle touches. He told him that the blaring band and the great crowd that hailed the post parade were nothing to get excited about. He reminded him of other races, other crowds.

Henry said, "One thing's sure. At a mile and a quarter the ground won't run out on him."

The Black rose high in the air and came down hard against Napoleon. Alec kept his seat and held him close.

Remember when we didn't have Napoleon? he asked his horse. *You'd get excited and reach for the sky. I'd go up and be lucky to find you on the way down.*

Henry said, "Still, if it was a shorter race I wouldn't be so worried about his handlin' the weight."

The Black sought to get closer to Casey but Alec kept him back, bowing the stallion's neck with shortened rein.

Remember Sagr? Casey is the same golden color, isn't he? Some day we'll go back to Arabia, you and I. Maybe we'll even race Sagr again!

The band burst forth in a loud and brassy march. The Black jumped and Alec slid with him.

Remember the high booming pitch of the Bedouin drums just before the desert race? They really made noise! Lots more noise than this but for the same reason.

Behind the fence rail spectators jumped up and down, trying to see over the heads of those in front. They shouted at the top of their lungs and the Black's ears turned toward them.

Remember how the tribesmen began to dance while all the women and children clapped their hands and chanted? They shouted and whistled and hissed through their teeth while the men stamped their feet upon the ground and the dust rose about their bodies so we could hardly see them.

Henry said, "I put as much of the lead as possible up in the front pockets of the pad. I wanted it up near the withers where he can carry it best."

A quarter of a mile up the homestretch the starting gate awaited them. The stall doors were open and the ground crew was ready to take the three horses inside. High on his platform the official starter waited, patient and smiling. Between the Black's pricked ears Alec watched him.

Remember that old chieftain who started us off, Sheikh somebody or other? Boy, was he old! I'll bet he was over a hundred, he was so wrinkled. He didn't wear a white robe like most of the others. He had a red headdress and a red flowing gown.

Henry said, "If it was any horse but the Black I'd take you off and put a heavier rider up. I don't like to carry so much 'dead' weight. We've got almost forty pounds of it."

Still smiling, the official starter called through his amplifier, "No, hurry, boys. We've all the time in the world." Everybody knew he was joking, and that he was worried stiff about getting this big race off to a bad start.

Remember how the little old man smiled? More with his eyes than his mouth. He truly smiled, not like the man up there on the platform. When he raised his hand the shouting and the drums stopped. Everybody just watched his hand, including me. When it dropped we went.

The Black slid away from Napoleon and Henry said, "There's nothin' I can tell you, Alec. Keep out of trouble and keep goin'. That's about it. He'll run for you until he's out of gas. With the weight he's carryin' I don't know when that'll be. I'm hopin' it won't be before a mile and a quarter."

His hand slipped from the boy's shoulder to the old saddle and stayed there until a crewman beckoned Alec to bring the

Black forward into his starting box. "You got everything, Alec," the trainer said, "—the best there is."

Alec remained quiet and his face was as set as a piece of carved mahogany. Henry understood the boy's long silence. It had been no different for him many years ago.

"Easy, Mister," Alec said aloud while taking the Black into his stall. "Easy now. It's just another race, that's all it is. A race is a race wherever it might be."

Like the official starter he talked just to hear himself talk. He wasn't fooling anyone, not even himself. No two races were ever alike, and this was the Black beneath him.

The Brooklyn Handicap

19

Now there was no past, no other race. Nothing but the one to come, with the three of them in a row waiting for the door flaps to spring open and set them free.

Don't break him too fast from the gate, Alec cautioned himself. *Let him come out slow, if he likes, until he finds his stride. Then let him run. You know better than anyone else what you have under you. No lead weights can beat a horse like him.*

The Black stood perfectly still as if well aware of what it was all about. Even his ears were pitched forward, all ready to go.

Alec felt the heavy strips of lead beneath his knees. Most of the weight was where Henry had wanted it, forward on the withers. The pad was buckled down tight. It would not slip forward or backward or from side to side. It would stay put while the Black was in full run. Alec believed that a weighted pad was less harmful to a running horse than a heavy rider who was apt to become unbalanced. Moving forward, he placed his weight too over the Black's withers. Now, very still and crouched low in the saddle, he waited with his horse.

To the Black's left was Casey, hot and nervous and anxious to be turned loose from the confinement of his narrow stall. Casey, the favorite son of New York fans because he seldom raced anywhere else and therefore belonged to them alone. They'd sympathized with him in his physical ailments as a two- and three-year-old when, despite his early speed, he had not been a very impressive looking animal. However, they were sure that if it had not been for his aching hoofs, which could be likened to their own feet with their troublesome corns and bunions, he would have been a great colt.

Their prophecy proved correct the following year when Casey reached full maturity and became a striking and statuesque horse with a gleaming, golden coat. His feet remained sound and he put on show after show, rocketing from behind a packed field with an explosive flourish that took him to victory after victory and endeared him forever to New York racing fans. They truly loved him, and today they looked with concerned eyes upon the two big stars on either side of him . . . not that they thought for a moment that Casey had anything to fear.

They watched Eclipse fuss a bit in the first stall and then become quiet. No three-year-old in the history of racing had so completely dominated his age division as this big colt. And certainly none had left his age group to blow down older horses so gustily as he had done a few weeks ago. Yet he was very lightly weighted. It was enough to make anyone worry just a bit.

Eclipse they knew well and what to expect from him. But the Black? His comeback had been very slow and careful, just one sprint race, really, if one discounted the race in which Billy Watts's accident had occurred. They'd seen many such horses beaten by race-hardened competitors. Training schedules lacked the intangible benefits that only races could provide.

Still, hadn't they doffed their hats to him when he'd "bulled" his way through a hole which wasn't big enough in the Speed Handicap? If that was truly the kind of heart he had and he showed it again today, he might possibly make a race of it with Casey.

Unlike Casey's avid fans the impartial horsemen who waited for the gate to open looked upon the three stars in a far different light. They had no favorites. All three horses possessed the versatility that greatness demands of champions. Each had proven he could sprint or stay. Each could set a blistering pace and hold it or race from far back, waiting until the very white of the finish line shone in his eyes before throwing on full power.

What then would be the strategy of the men who rode these horses? Who would send his mount to the front and set the pace? Would it be Ted Robinson on Eclipse in a blazing attempt to wear down Casey and the Black under their heavy weights? If so, would Mike Costello and Alec Ramsay let the big colt go off without attempting to catch him? Many horses had come to grief trying to chase the speedy Eclipse in the early stages of a race. Would they hold back their mounts waiting for Eclipse to expend much of his energy before setting out to catch him? A race was won by one or several short bursts of speed, which might come at the beginning, middle or end. Never was top speed sustained too long, for no horse is capable of going all out for more than a quarter of a mile. The horses would do the running but what about the hands that guided them? Who held the victory?

Alec rubbed the Black's shoulders but there was no need to quiet his horse. Never had he stood so still! For a second Alec was afraid that something might be wrong. But the Black had cleaned his feedbox that morning. He'd walked soundly. He'd taken the short van ride from Belmont Park to Aqueduct without undue fussing and he hadn't had to stay very long in the receiving barn before going to the paddock.

Suddenly Casey rose in the air and everybody had to wait for him to come down and get straightened out again.

"'Tis no chance, sir!" Michael Costello shouted to the starter. "No chance at all!"

The Black snorted at all the commotion on his left and then he, too, went up in the air. Alec brought him down, relieved that the Black was acting more like himself.

"I'm going to hold you back as much as you'll take without getting mad at me," he told him. "Then I'll let you run."

The Black had quieted down again. He was too still for the break about to come and Alec slapped him lightly on the neck. "Don't go falling asleep on me now. The guy upstairs is ready to push the button. We're on our way. I know it."

Alec looked straight down the long, empty homestretch. It would look a lot longer the next time around when the Black would feel most of his heavy burden of 146 pounds. Out of the corner of his eyes, Alec saw Casey start to go up again. Mike pulled the chestnut horse down and as he did Casey's left foreleg struck the door. It opened as it was designed to do when struck as a safety precaution. *Almost at that precise second the other doors sprang open too!* The starter had pushed the button and the "Race of the Century" was on!

Casey had a jump on them, Alec saw as he turned the Black loose. Another jump and Casey was clear of trouble with nothing to fear from either Eclipse or the Black. Alec made no attempt to go after him. Without hurrying the Black he waited for him to settle in stride.

Eclipse was being sent after Casey, Robinson's face showing his surprise at Mike Costello's determination to stay in front. Alec too was surprised when Mike went for his whip, sending Casey along at a faster clip until he was far enough ahead of Eclipse to move over to the rail.

The crowd roared its approval of Casey's unpredicted early sprint as the horses swept down the quarter-mile stretch to the finish line and then began their trip around the mile track.

Alec let the Black settle into third place, content to remain there until the time came to make his move. Unlike either of the other riders he had not planned a front run with his horse. To win, the Black must wear the others down at the proper time, probably in the final eighth of a mile. It was still a long way off.

The Black began to eat away at the margin between him and Eclipse. Alec inched up the reins a bit more, restraining his horse. He was pleased with the way the race was going. He'd never expected Casey to be the pacesetter. Now he could let Casey soften up Eclipse in a sprinting duel up front. They'd be shining marks for a comparatively fresh Black in the long homestretch.

The wet leather slipped a little in Alec's hands when they swept into the first turn. It was getting more difficult to restrain the Black without making him mad, but Alec felt confident he could do it as long as he didn't have to slow him up much more. They were five lengths behind the others with Casey still setting a blistering pace and Eclipse following directly in his wake. It seemed that Ted Robinson was now content to let Mike Costello set the pace, for he was making no effort to pass him. The race was still going as Alec wanted it.

A few seconds later the Black began closing up on the leaders by half the distance! By the middle of the sharp turn he was nearing Eclipse's hindquarters! Alec wound the reins around his hands and the Black shook his head, seeking relief from the abruptly tightened lines.

Alec guided him to the right of Eclipse but managed to stay behind. He didn't want to pass for he knew now that Mike Costello's strategy had not been to take the lead to kill off his opposition *but to set as slow a pace as possible*. Mike intended to do all he could to have a fresh mount for the stretch run despite Casey's high impost of 136 pounds.

Ted Robinson did not yet realize how greatly the pace had been slowed, Alec knew. There was no concern on his face. Following so close on Casey's heels Robinson had no idea that the old jockey up front had skillfully and gradually shortened Eclipse's strides as well as those of his own mount. If Alec had not been far enough back to use the gap between them as a yardstick he might not have known it either.

It was an old trick but always good when executed with finesse. Mike Costello had done it to perfection. There had been no sudden and noticeable slackening of speed going around the turn. Now he was still setting a slow pace while Eclipse and the Black trailed him.

Except for the Black's mounting fury at being held back, Alec was not unhappy with Mike's strategy. What worked for Casey would work for the Black too. Only Eclipse would

suffer from the slow, easy pace. The light-weighted colt
might have worn them down by going to the front and
maintaining a sustained drive to the very end, giving them
no chance to rest their horses. They would have had to catch
Eclipse to beat him.

The Black pushed his head harder against the bit and
snorted repeatedly. Ted Robinson glanced back but made no
attempt to pull Eclipse out from the rail and pass Casey. He
seemed completely unaware of what had happened to the
pace.

Up front Mike Costello never turned his head but Alec
imagined the wiry Irishman had his ears tuned to the hoof-
beats behind him. If they moved up on him he'd send Casey
along a little faster to stay on top. But he wouldn't budge
until then. Alec snugged up the reins still more to keep the
Black from passing Eclipse. He was in an excellent position
to make his bid and there was no hurry—no hurry at all.

Coming off the turn and entering the long backstretch,
they completed the first half-mile of the race with three-quarters to go. When they passed the pole, Alec saw Ted Robinson glance at his hands. He knew then that Eclipse's jockey
was riding with a stopwatch.

Mike's trick was over!

Alec got ready to go with the Black. Never had he held
him back so long and so hard. The leather seemed to be im-
bedded in his hands. This kind of restraint had been no part
of his plans, for he'd intended to hold back only as much as
the Black would take kindly!

Robinson reacted quickly to the slow time. He slapped
Eclipse sharply and the big, burly colt jumped from behind
Casey and came around. Alec pulled the Black over to the
right to avoid Eclipse's charge and in doing so had to take

him up still more. In front Mike Costello knew that his ruse had failed; he sent Casey along faster, trying to keep the lead from Eclipse. Now the race to the very finish was on!

As the other two horses lengthened their strides the Black shook his head furiously. Alec realized that his last tug on the reins had shattered whatever patience the stallion had left. Angered and frustrated by the prolonged restraint the Black suddenly bolted out of control! Instead of going after the others he swerved sharply, twisting his head and body to free himself of rein and bit and hands!

Alec swung with his horse, trying to stay in the saddle. The Black came down hard and the force of it sent his rider onto the stallion's neck, his hands seeking a hold in the black mane. For the first time the reins were loose.

The Black bolted again and Alec lurched with him, going forward then backward into the saddle. There he stayed while the Black set out after the others, running free as he'd wanted to do all along.

Many lengths beyond, Robinson was rocking wildly on Eclipse. The thick-bodied colt surged past Casey, taking the rail and the lead. Mike Costello had no alternative but to follow the vigorous pace being forced upon him. He let Casey out several notches for he couldn't allow the colt to draw too far away, not with only 116 pounds on his back.

Now the Black, too, was in full flight, his head stretched out and nostrils snorting as if he were overjoyed by his newly won freedom. Alec took up the reins but made no attempt to shorten them. The distance between them and the hard-running leaders began to close. Alec knew that Eclipse would be kept in a sustained drive until the very end. There'd be no short bursts of speed, no chance to rest in between and make the Black's heavy burden easier to bear in that final eighth of a mile. But what was happening to them was happening to Casey and Mike as well. They had no alternative now but to go after Eclipse. They had to catch the flying colt to beat him.

Alec urged the Black on with his voice but the rest of him was deathly still—still and forward, where 146 pounds would be the easiest to take.

In a way he, too, was glad the waiting was over, regardless of what it might cost in the end. He watched the gap close, narrowing more and more with each of the Black's strides. This race was not like any other race. This was not simply a case of one horse finishing in front of other horses. This was one to remember as long as there were horses and racing. The two leaders were going faster and faster, and now the Black gained upon them by inches rather than feet.

Three in a row, one behind the other, they swept into the sharp far turn. Their riders knew that the backstretch run at top speed had done damage to them all. And there was still a half-mile to go.

Eclipse's strides were steady but they did not come quite so effortlessly as before. Casey followed doggedly with much of his speed and stamina wrung out of him. The Black drew a little closer to them but it was like a man pulling himself up a rope with only his hands. The pace and weight were beginning to tell on him too.

Alec moved the Black nearer to the rail, the shortest path available to the wire. He took up on the reins a little, trying to check their speed to give his horse a short rest before entering that long, heartrending stretch.

The black stallion shook his head vigorously at the slight pull on the reins. There would be no resting the Black, Alec realized. His horse was going all-out to the finish because that was the kind of heart he had.

But Eclipse and Casey were not lacking in heart either. Like the champions they were there was no slackening of stride as they came off the turn with still more than a quarter of a mile to go. They were displaying speed and stamina and now came the final test of courage!

Alec stopped talking to the Black, knowing nothing he could say would help his horse catch the others. He remained very still and sat forward and low in the saddle, trying only to ease the Black's heavy burden. Now with every stride the weight became greater. Alec felt the extra leaden pounds in his horse's every movement. No longer was the Black running without pain.

The great stands loomed to the right of the track and there was less than a quarter of a mile to go. Eclipse was not yet a spent horse and his sustained drive continued through the stretch while the spectators roared. But their calls were not for him—they were for Casey, who drew laboriously up to Eclipse's flanks. Behind them the Black was skimming the rail and slowly eating away at the margin they held over him.

At the last furlong pole with two hundred and twenty yards to go Eclipse looked the winner to the frenzied crowd. Casey and the Black were cutting his lead down inch by inch but the ground was running out on them! There wasn't time to *inch up* on the flying leader. The crowd knew Eclipse would have been a beaten horse at level weights but this was a handicap and the horses were coming down to the wire three in a row!

Alec swung the Black from the rail without loss of stride.

The shortest path to the wire was no longer the fastest with Eclipse and Casey running there. He took his horse to the outside, knowing it cost him several of the bitterly fought inches the Black had earned. But the path to the wire was clear before them and the Black surged forward again, his breath and strides coming hard. Air as well as ground was running out on him. He inched forward as did Casey until the finish wire shone bright in the eyes of all three horses and their riders.

They were so closely bunched that they could have been covered by a large rug. Among all the tumultuous thousands who watched, only one person remained quiet. He was an old man with sparse white hair who held his hat in his hands to keep them from shaking. He watched Casey and Eclipse racing head to head, nose to nose. He was aware of the oncoming black stallion, whose rider sat so still, asking nothing because his horse was giving everything. He knew further that the Black's final drive was not to be denied, that his determination to get up with the others was as unyielding as the result of this race was unalterable. Suddenly he, too, screamed at the top of his voice!

Alec felt the quick gathering of the Black's body. Then came a tremendous surge and his horse was alongside Casey and Eclipse! Another jump and the Black's head went to the front while above them flashed the finish wire!

"Pshaw!" said the old man in the stands. "If I'd given him another pound, I would have had it."

Black-Out

20

The Black knew the race was over, for his long strides slowed heavily without Alec's bidding. He went all the way to the turn and around it before finally coming to a halt. He stood in the center of the track, his eyes on the infield's soft green grass rather than the roaring stands beyond.

Finally, at Alec's request, he turned and went back. There was no doubt that he was terribly tired, for he moved at a very slow pace. Yet his breathing was regular and came without effort. To the thousands awaiting him he probably looked disinterested, as if he'd just finished a routine work. Alec knew differently. It had taken every bit of the Black's great heart and courage to win this race.

Gently stroking his horse, Alec could feel the multitude of blood vessels, tiny under normal circumstances but now raised and bulging beneath his wet hands. He would have liked to help the Black by dismounting, but according to the rules he wasn't allowed to until he was given permission by the judges. With dismay he looked ahead at the jammed throng awaiting them at the winner's circle.

"I'll get you out of there soon," he promised his horse. "You've done plenty just winning this one."

The news photographers overflowed the winner's enclosure and began taking pictures while Alec and the Black were still on the track. Henry came forward and took hold of the stallion's bridle. Amid all the noise and confusion the trainer said nothing but his eyes spoke eloquently for him as he looked with wondrous pride upon horse and rider.

Alec called, "He's real tired, Henry. Let's make this short."

A moment later they were within the circle and Alec overheard Mike Costello say into the television and radio microphones, " 'Tis no excuse we have today but the Black."

More pictures were being taken and Alec looked hopefully toward the judges' stand for permission to dismount. Not until the tired Black struck out at the photographers did the signal come for Alec to dismount. Gratefully he slid off his horse and unsaddled him. Carrying his tack, he stepped onto the scales in the enclosure.

"One hundred forty-six pounds. Check," said the Clerk. Only then was the Brooklyn Handicap officially over and the news of the Black's winning flashed around the world.

Now the crowd pressed closer and Alec tried to return to his horse. Television crews stopped him and over their heads he saw the Black strike out with his hind legs again, making room for himself. Henry held the reins with one hand and with the other accepted a silver dish from a dignified-looking mayor who kept a wary eye on the Black during the brief ceremony.

The television interviewer put his arm around Alec, pulling him into camera range. "Alec. Alec Ramsay," he said, with great flourish. "Congratulations on a great victory! Now, you're one of the few riders who can come back with a winner and tell us something about him. How'd it feel to be coming down that stretch? We've never seen a more relentless drive than he put on during that last eighth of a mile. It seemed to us that the Black was undaunted, that he would have worn the others down at any cost! Did you feel it too?"

Alec nodded while looking anxiously at the Black. "I knew he'd overtake them but I wasn't sure he'd catch them in time," he said.

"What a finish it was! You know, of course, that Eclipse and Casey finished in a dead heat?"

Alec nodded. "They were nose to nose when we jumped by. It was a great job of handicapping, although no one knew it until now."

"It'll go down as the most *sensational* finish, the most *famous,* the most *remembered* of all races!" the interviewer said grandly.

Alec started to leave but the man grabbed his arm. "Just one thing more, Alec, please. What's ahead of you now?"

"Offhand I'd say building a new barn," Alec answered, smiling. "And just as fireproof as we can make it."

"Yes, yes, we know about that," the interviewer said impatiently, "but what about racing the Black again?"

Alec said, "You'd better ask Henry." As he went toward his horse the interviewer, complete with microphone and cables and camera, followed in his wake.

Alec took the Black from Henry. "I'll get him out of here while you take care of this guy," he said. As Alec was carefully leading the Black from the enclosure he heard the high shrill voice of the television man.

"Henry, Henry Dailey! Congratulations on the training of

a great horse! But a great horse can be a problem sometimes. He runs out of competition unless you accept new challenges such as the big international races in foreign countries—England's *Ascot Gold Cup,* France's *Prix de l'Arc de Triomphe,* Italy's—"

"Now whatya know!" Henry exclaimed. "That's not such a bad idea at that. Why, we might even get a break in the weights! But right now I've got a horse to cool off. So long, everybody!"

The screen on television sets throughout the country showed Henry Dailey running through the crowd after Alec Ramsay and the Black. The viewers, as well as those left standing in the winner's circle, would have liked to see his face. If they had seen it, they might have been able to tell how serious he was about racing the Black abroad. As the interviewer had said, *there should always be new challenges ahead, even for the Black.*

ABOUT THE AUTHOR

WALTER FARLEY's love of horses began when he was a small boy living in Syracuse, New York, and continued when his family moved to New York City. Unlike most city children, he was able to fulfill this love through an uncle who was a professional horseman. Young Walter spent much of his time with this uncle, learning about the different kinds of horse training and the people associated with each.

Walter Farley began to write his first book, *The Black Stallion*, when he was in high school. He finished it and had it published in 1941 while he was still an undergraduate at Columbia University. The appearance of *The Black Stallion* brought such an enthusiastic response from young readers that Mr. Farley went on to create more stories about the Black, and about other horses as well. In his life he wrote a total of thirty-four titles. His books have been enormously popular in the United States and have been published in twenty-one foreign countries.

Mr. Farley and his wife, Rosemary, had four children— Pam, Alice, Steve, and Tim—whom they raised on a farm in Pennsylvania and in a beach house in Florida. Horses, dogs, and cats were always part of the household. In 1968 Pam Farley was killed in a car crash in Europe at the age of twenty. Mr. Farley memorialized her free spirit and love of horses in *The Black Stallion and the Girl*, and expressed his abiding grief in *The Black Stallion Legend*.

In 1989 Mr. Farley was honored by his hometown library in Venice, Florida, which established the Walter Farley Literary Landmark in its children's wing. Mr. Farley died in October 1989, shortly before publication of *The Young Black Stallion*, the twenty-first book in the Black Stallion series.

Shipwrecked!

The Black Stallion

by Walter Farley

When young Alec Ramsay first sees the huge black stallion in the cargo hold of the *Drake*, he can tell that the Black is an exceptional horse. Then the *Drake* is shipwrecked, and the stallion saves Alec's life! Stranded on a desert island, boy and stallion develop a special bond. The Black is all the horse that Alec has ever dreamed of, and more. Determined to win this great beast's trust and love, Alec sets out to tame him. But the job turns out to be more exciting—and more dangerous— than Alec could ever have imagined....

"The Black Stallion is about the most famous fictional horse of the century."
—*New York Times*

A BULLSEYE BOOK PUBLISHED BY ALFRED A. KNOPF, INC.

No girls allowed!

The Black Stallion and the Girl

by Walter Farley

When a pretty girl answers his ad for an experienced stable hand, Alec is a bit surprised. Petite, gentle, and free-spirited, Pam is not exactly what Alec had in mind for the job. But her easy way with the horses quickly wins her Alec's respect—and the job.

But Henry is not so easily convinced. The trainer is a member of the old school of horse racing, and he firmly believes that girls have no place in the business. And because he is a part owner of Hopeful Farm, his opinion counts. Will Alec be forced to choose between the girl who's won his heart and the horseman who's always had his trust?

"Everyone loves a champion. And when the champion is a gallant horse, when his story is told by a champion of horse stories, every reader is a winner."

—*New York Times*

A BULLSEYE BOOK PUBLISHED BY ALFRED A. KNOPF, INC.

The Black must be saved!

The Black Stallion Returns

by Walter Farley

Someone is determined to pull Alec and the Black apart. First Alec finds deadly poison in the Black's stable. Then, while he's trying to track down the culprit, an Arabian chieftain shows up and reclaims the Black. Alec is convinced that these two events are part of the same mystery and that the answer lies somewhere deep in Arabia. Determined to protect his beloved horse from harm, Alec sets off on an adventure that takes him halfway around the world. Across scorching desert sands Alec trails the Black through an exotic world of evil and intrigue.

"Walter Farley writes with a warm understanding of horses and the men who train and ride them. He deserves his top-favorite position with horse story readers."

—*Chicago Sunday Tribune*

A BULLSEYE BOOK PUBLISHED BY ALFRED A. KNOPF, INC.